The Pursuit of
The House-Boat

*Being Some Further Account of the Divers
Doings of the Associated Shades, under the
Leadership of Sherlock Holmes, Esq.*

By

John Kendrick Bangs

Illustrated

By Peter Newell

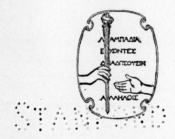

New York and London

Harper & Brothers

Publishers 1902

CONTENTS

CHAP.   PAGE
   I. THE ASSOCIATED SHADES TAKE ACTION   1

  II. THE STRANGER UNRAVELS A MYSTERY

        AND REVEALS HIMSELF 18

 III. THE SEARCH-PARTY IS ORGANIZED . 42

  IV. ON BOARD THE HOUSE-BOAT . . . 58

   V. A CONFERENCE ON DECK 73

  VI. A CONFERENCE BELOW-STAIRS . . 89

 VII. THE "GEHENNA" IS CHARTERED. . 105

VIII. ON BOARD THE "GEHENNA." . . . 121

  IX. CAPTAIN KIDD MEETS WITH AN OB-

        STACLE 139

   X. A WARNING ACCEPTED 157

  XI. MAROONED 172

 XII. THE ESCAPE AND THE END. . . . 189

ILLUSTRATIONS

"THE STRANGER DREW FORTH A BUNDLE OF
BUSINESS CARDS" . . . . *Frontispiece*

"'DR. JOHNSON'S POINT IS WELL TAKEN'" . *Facing p.* 8

"'WHAT HAS ALL THIS GOT TO DO WITH
THE QUESTION?'" . . . . " 10

"POOR OLD BOSWELL WAS PUSHED OVER-
BOARD" . . . . " 22

"THREE ROUSING CHEERS, LED BY HAMLET,
WERE GIVEN" . . . . " 42

A BLACK PERSON BY THE NAME OF FRIDAY
FINDS A BOTTLE . . . . " 54

MADAME RÉCAMIER HAS A PLAN . . . . " 66

"THE HARD FEATURES OF KIDD WERE THRUST
THROUGH". . . . . " 70

"'HERE'S A KETTLE OF FISH,' SAID KIDD" . " 74

"'EVERY BLOOMIN' MILLION WAS REPRESENT-
ED BY A CERTIFIED CHECK, AN' PAYA-
BLE IN LONDON'" . . . . " 84

QUEEN ELIZABETH DESIRES AN AXE AND ONE
HOUR OF HER OLDEN POWER . . . . " 90

"'THE COMMITTEE ON TREACHERY IS READY
    TO REPORT'" . . . . *Facing p.* 102

"'YOU ARE VERY MUCH MISTAKEN, SIR
    WALTER'" . . . . "   108

"IN THE DEAD OF NIGHT SHYLOCK HAD
    STOLEN UP THE GANG-PLANK" . . . "   118

JUDGE BLACKSTONE REFUSES TO CLIMB TO
    THE MIZZENTOP . . . . "   126

SHEM IN THE LOOKOUT . . . . "   128

CAPTAIN KIDD CONSENTS TO BE CROSS-EX-
    AMINED BY PORTIA . . . . "   148

KIDD'S COMPANIONS ENDEAVORING TO RE-
    STORE EVAPORATED PORTIONS OF HIS
    ANATOMY WITH A STEAM-ATOMIZER   . "   154

"'HE TOLD US WE WERE GOING TO PARIS'" "   160

"'YOU ARE A VERY CLEAR-HEADED YOUNG
    WOMAN, LIZZIE,' SAID MRS. NOAH"   · "   170

"'THAT OUGHT TO BE A LESSON TO YOU'" "   178

"THE PIRATES MADE A MAD DASH DOWN THE
    ROUGH, ROCKY HILL-SIDE" . . . . "   180

"'NOW, MY CHILD,' SAID MRS. NOAH, FIRMLY,
    'I DO NOT WISH ANY WORDS'" . . "   192

"A GREAT HELPLESS HULK TEN FEET TO
    THE REAR" . . . . "   200

THE PURSUIT OF THE HOUSE-BOAT

THE PURSUIT

THE HOUSE-BOAT

I

THE ASSOCIATED SHADES TAKE ACTION

THE House-boat of the Associated
Shades, formerly located upon the River
Styx, as the reader may possibly remember, had been torn from its moorings and
navigated out into unknown seas by that
vengeful pirate Captain Kidd, aided and
abetted by some of the most ruffianly inhabitants of Hades. Like a thief in the
night had they come, and for no better
reason than that the Captain had been
unanimously voted a shade too shady to

associate with self-respecting spirits had they made off with the happy floating club-house of their betters; and worst of all, with them, by force of circumstances over which they had no control, had sailed also the fair Queen Elizabeth, the spirited Xanthippe, and every other strong-minded and beautiful woman of Erebean society, whereby the men thereof were rendered desolate.

"I can't stand it !" cried Raleigh, desperately, as with his accustomed grace he presided over a special meeting of the club, called on the bank of the inky Stygian stream, at the point where the missing boat had been moored. "Think of it, gentlemen, Elizabeth of England, Calpurnia of Rome, Ophelia of Denmark, and every precious jewel in our social diadem gone, vanished completely; and with whom ?   Kidd, of all men in the universe! Kidd, the pirate, the ruffian—"

"Don't take on so, my dear Sir Walter," said Socrates, cheerfully.   "What's the use of going into hysterics ?   You are not a woman, and should eschew that luxury. Xanthippe is with them, and I'll warrant you that when that cherished spouse of mine has recovered from the effects of the sea, say the third day out, Kidd and his crew will be walking the plank, and voluntarily at that."

"But the House-boat itself," murmured Noah, sadly. "That was my delight. It reminded me in some respects of the Ark."

"The law of compensation enters in there, my dear Commodore," retorted Socrates. "For me, with Xanthippe abroad I do not need a club to go to; I can stay at home and take my hemlock in peace and straight. Xanthippe always compelled me to dilute it at the rate of one quart of water to the finger."

"Well, we didn't all marry Xanthippe," put in Cæsar, firmly, "therefore we are not all satisfied with the situation. I, for one, quite agree with Sir Walter that something must be done, and quickly. Are we to sit here and do nothing, allow-ing that fiend to kidnap our wives with impunity?"

"Not at all," interposed Bonaparte. "The time for action has arrived. All things considered he is welcome to Marie Louise, but the idea of Josephine going off on a cruise of that kind breaks my heart."

"No question about it," observed Dr. Johnson. "We've got to do something if it is only for the sake of appearances. The question really is, what shall be done first?"

"I am in favor of taking a drink as the first step, and considering the matter of further action afterwards," suggested Shakespeare, and it was this suggestion that made the members unanimous upon the necessity for immediate action, for when the assembled spirits called for their various favorite beverages it was found that there were none to be had, it being Sunday, and all the establishments wherein liquid refreshments were licensed to be sold being closed—for at the time of writing the local government of Hades was in the hands of the reform party.

"What!" cried Socrates. "Nothing but Styx water and vitriol, Sundays? Then the House-boat must be recovered whether Xanthippe comes with it or not. Sir Walter, I am for immediate action, after all. This ruffian should be captured at once and made an example of."

"Excuse me, Socrates," put in Lindley Murray, "but, ah—pray speak in Greek hereafter, will you, please? When you attempt English you have a beastly way of working up to climatic prepositions which are offensive to the ear of a purist."

"This is no time to discuss style, Murray," interposed Sir Walter. "Socrates may speak and spell like Chaucer if he pleases; he may even part his infinitives in the middle, for all I care. We have affairs of greater moment in hand."

"We must ransack the earth," cried Socrates, "until we find that boat. I'm dry as a fish."

"There he goes again!" growled Murray. "Dry as a fish! What fish I'd like to know is dry?"

"Red herrings," retorted Socrates; and there was a great laugh at the expense of the purist, in which even Hamlet, who had grown more and more melancholy and morbid since the abduction of Ophelia, joined.

"Then it is settled," said Raleigh; "something must be done. And now the point is, what?"

"Relief expeditions have a way of finding things," suggested Dr. Livingstone. "Or rather of being found by the things they go out to relieve. I propose that we send out a number of them. I will take Africa; Bonaparte can lead an expedition into Europe; General Washington may have North America; and—"

"I beg pardon," put in Dr. Johnson, "but have you any idea, Dr. Livingstone, that Captain Kidd has put wheels on this House-boat of ours and is having it dragged across the Sahara by mules or camels?"

"No such absurd idea ever entered my head," retorted the Doctor.

"Do you then believe that he has put runners on it, and is engaged in the pleasurable pastime of taking the ladies tobogganing down the Alps?" persisted the philosopher.

"Not at all. Why do you ask?" queried the African explorer, irritably.

"Because I wish to know," said Johnson. "That is always my motive in asking questions. You propose to go looking for a house-boat in Central Africa; you suggest that Bonaparte lead an expedition in search of it through Europe —all of which strikes me as nonsense. This search is the work of sea-dogs, not of landlubbers. You might as well ask Confucius to look for it in the heart of China. What earthly use there is in ransacking the earth I fail to see. What we need is a naval expedition to scour the sea, unless it is pretty well understood in advance that we believe Kidd has hauled the boat out of the water, and is now

using it for a roller-skating rink or a bi-
cycle academy in Ohio, or for some other
purpose for which neither he nor it was
designed."

"Dr. Johnson's point is well taken,"
said a stranger who had been sitting upon
the string-piece of the pier, quietly, but
with very evident interest, listening to
the discussion. He was a tall and excessively slender shade, "like a spirt of steam
out of a teapot," as Johnson put it afterwards, so slight he seemed. "I have not
the honor of being a member of this association," the stranger continued, "but,
like all well - ordered shades, I aspire to
the distinction, and I hold myself and my
talents at the disposal of this club. I
fancy it will not take us long to establish
our initial point, which is that the gross
person who has so foully appropriated
your property to his own base uses does
not contemplate removing it from its keel
and placing it somewhere inland. All
the evidence in hand points to a radically
different conclusion, which is my sole rea-

"'DR. JOHNSON'S POINT IS WELL TAKEN'"

son for doubting the value of that conclusion. Captain Kidd is a seafarer by
instinct, not a landsman. The House-
boat is not a house, but a boat; therefore
the place to look for it is not, as Dr. Johnson so well says, in the Sahara Desert, or
on the Alps, or in the State of Ohio, but
upon the high sea, or upon the water-
front of some one of the world's great
cities."

"And what, then, would be your plan?"
asked Sir Walter, impressed by the stranger's manner as well as by the very manifest reason in all that he had said.

"The chartering of a suitable vessel,
fully armed and equipped for the purpose
of pursuit. Ascertain whither the House-
boat has sailed, for what port, and start
at once. Have you a model of the House-
boat within reach?" returned the stranger.

"I think not; we have the architect's
plans, however," said the chairman.

"We had, Mr. Chairman," said Demosthenes, who was secretary of the House

Committee, rising, "but they are gone with the House-boat itself. They were kept in the safe in the hold."

A look of annoyance came into the face of the stranger.

"That's too bad," he said. "It was a most important part of my plan that we should know about how fast the House-boat was."

"Humph!" ejaculated Socrates, with ill-concealed sarcasm. "If you'll take Xanthippe's word for it, the House-boat was the fastest yacht afloat."

"I refer to the matter of speed in sailing," returned the stranger, quietly. "The question of its ethical speed has nothing to do with it."

"The designer of the craft is here," said Sir Walter, fixing his eyes upon Sir Christopher Wren. "It is possible that he may be of assistance in settling that point."

"What has all this got to do with the question, anyhow, Mr. Chairman?" asked Solomon, rising impatiently and address-

"'WHAT HAS ALL THIS GOT TO DO WITH THE QUESTION?'"

ing Sir Walter. "We aren't preparing
for a yacht-race that I know of. Nobody's after a cup, or a championship of
any kind. What we do want is to get our
wives back. The Captain hasn't taken
more than half of mine along with him,
but I am interested none the less. The
Queen of Sheba is on board, and I am
somewhat interested in her fate. So I
ask you what earthly or unearthly use
there is in discussing this question of
speed in the House-boat. It strikes me
as a woful waste of time, and rather un-
precedented too, that we should suspend
all rules and listen to the talk of an entire
stranger."

"I do not venture to doubt the wisdom
of Solomon," said Johnson, dryly, "but
I must say that the gentleman's remarks
rather interest me."

"Of course they do," ejaculated Solomon. "He agreed with you. That
ought to make him interesting to everybody. Freaks usually are."

"That is not the reason at all," retorted Dr. Johnson. "Cold water agrees with me, but it doesn't interest me. What I do think, however, is that our unknown friend seems to have a grasp on the situation by which we are confronted, and he's going at the matter in hand in a very comprehensive fashion. I move, therefore, that Solomon be laid on the table, and that the privileges of the—ah—of the wharf be extended indefinitely to our friend on the string-piece."

The motion, having been seconded, was duly carried, and the stranger resumed.

"I will explain for the benefit of his Majesty King Solomon, whose wisdom I have always admired, and whose endurance as the husband of three hundred wives has filled me with wonder," he said, "that before starting in pursuit of the stolen vessel we must select a craft of some sort for the purpose, and that in selecting the pursuer it is quite essential that we should choose a vessel of greater speed than the one we desire to overtake. It would hardly be proper, I think, if the

House-boat can sail four knots an hour, to attempt to overhaul her with a launch, or other nautical craft, with a maximum speed of two knots an hour."

"Hear! hear!" ejaculated Cæsar.

"That is my reason, your Majesty, for inquiring as to the speed of your late club - house," said the stranger, bowing courteously to Solomon. "Now if Sir Christopher Wren can give me her measurements, we can very soon determine at about what rate she is leaving us behind under favorable circumstances."

"'Tisn't necessary for Sir Christopher to do anything of the sort," said Noah, rising and manifesting somewhat more heat than the occasion seemed to require. "As long as we are discussing the question I will take the liberty of stating what I have never mentioned before, that the designer of the House - boat merely appropriated the lines of the Ark. Shem, Ham, and Japhet will bear testimony to the truth of that statement."

"There can be no quarrel on that score,

Mr. Chairman," assented Sir Christopher, with cutting frigidity. "I am perfectly willing to admit that practically the two vessels were built on the same lines, but with modifications which would enable my boat to sail twenty miles to windward and back in six days less time than it would have taken the Ark to cover the same distance, and it could have taken all the wash of the excursion steamers into the bargain."

"Bosh!" ejaculated Noah, angrily. "Strip your old tub down to a flying balloon-jib and a marline-spike, and ballast the Ark with elephants until every inch of her reeked with ivory and peanuts, and she'd outfoot you on every leg, in a cyclone or a zephyr. Give me the Ark and a breeze, and your House-boat wouldn't be within hailing distance of her five minutes after the start if she had 40,000 square yards of canvas spread before a gale."

"This discussion is waxing very unprofitable," observed Confucius. "If

these gentlemen cannot be made to con-
fine themselves to the subject that is agi-
tating this body, I move we call in the
authorities and have them confined in the
bottomless pit."

"I did not precipitate the quarrel,"
said Noah. "I was merely trying to assist our friend on the string-piece. I was
going to say that as the Ark was probably
a hundred times faster than Sir Christopher Wren's—tub, which he himself says
can take care of all the wash of the excursion boats, thereby becoming on his own
admission a wash-tub—"

"Order! order!" cried Sir Christopher.

"I was going to say that this wash-tub
could be overhauled by a launch or any
other craft with a speed of thirty knots
a month," continued Noah, ignoring the
interruption.

"Took him forty days to get to Mount
Ararat!" sneered Sir Christopher.

"Well, your boat would have got there
two weeks sooner, I'll admit," retorted

Noah, " if she'd sprung a leak at the right time."

"Granting the truth of Noah's statement," said Sir Walter, motioning to the angry architect to be quiet—"not that we take any side in the issue between the two gentlemen, but merely for the sake of argument—I wish to ask the stranger who has been good enough to interest himself in our trouble what he proposes to do—how can you establish your course in case a boat were provided?"

"Also vot vill be dher gost, if any?" put in Shylock.

A murmur of disapprobation greeted this remark.

"The cost need not trouble you, sir," said Sir Walter, indignantly, addressing the stranger; "you will have carte blanche."

"Den ve are ruint!" cried Shylock, displaying his palms, and showing by that act a select assortment of diamond rings.

"Oh," laughed the stranger, "that is a

simple matter. Captain Kidd has gone to London."

"To London!" cried several members at once. "How do you know that?"

"By this," said the stranger, holding up the tiny stub end of a cigar.

"Tut-tut!" ejaculated Solomon. "What child's play this is!"

"No, your Majesty," observed the stranger, "it is not child's play; it is fact. That cigar end was thrown aside here on the wharf by Captain Kidd just before he stepped on board the House-boat."

"How do you know that?" demanded Raleigh. "And granting the truth of the assertion, what does it prove?"

"I will tell you," said the stranger. And he at once proceeded as follows.

II

THE STRANGER UNRAVELS A MYSTERY
AND REVEALS HIMSELF

"I HAVE made a hobby of the study of cigar ends," said the stranger, as the Associated Shades settled back to hear his account of himself. "From my earliest youth, when I used surreptitiously to remove the unsmoked ends of my father's cigars and break them up, and, in hiding, smoke them in an old clay pipe which I had presented to me by an ancient sea-captain of my acquaintance, I have been interested in tobacco in all forms, even including these self-same despised unsmoked ends; for they convey to my mind messages, sentiments, farces, comedies, and tragedies which to your minds would never become manifest through their agency."

The company drew closer together and
formed themselves in a more compact
mass about the speaker. It was evident
that they were beginning to feel an unusual interest in this extraordinary person,
who had come among them unheralded and
unknown. Even Shylock stopped calcu-
lating percentages for an instant to listen.

" Do you mean to tell us," demanded
Shakespeare, " that the unsmoked stub
of a cigar will suggest the story of him
who smoked it to your mind?"

" I do," replied the stranger, with a confident smile. " Take this one, for instance, that I have picked up here upon
the wharf; it tells me the whole story of
the intentions of Captain Kidd at the moment when, in utter disregard of your
rights, he stepped aboard your House-
boat, and, in his usual piratical fashion,
made off with it into unknown seas."

" But how do you know he smoked it?"
asked Solomon, who deemed it the part
of wisdom to be suspicious of the stranger.

" There are two curious indentations in

it which prove that. The marks of two
teeth, with a hiatus between, which you
will see if you look closely," said the
stranger, handing the small bit of tobacco
to Sir Walter, "make that point evident
beyond peradventure. The Captain lost
an eye-tooth in one of his later raids; it
was knocked out by a marline-spike which
had been hurled at him by one of the
crew of the treasure-ship he and his followers had attacked. The adjacent teeth
were broken, but not removed. The cigar end bears the marks of those two jag-
ged molars, with the hiatus, which, as I
have indicated, is due to the destruction
of the eye-tooth between them. It is not
likely that there was another man in the
pirate's crew with teeth exactly like the
commander's, therefore I say there can be
no doubt that the cigar end was that of
the Captain himself."

"Very interesting indeed," observed
Blackstone, removing his wig and fanning
himself with it; "but I must confess, Mr.
Chairman, that in any properly consti-

tuted law court this evidence would long since have been ruled out as irrelevant and absurd. The idea of two or three hundred dignified spirits like ourselves, gathered together to devise a means for the recovery of our property and the rescue of our wives, yielding the floor to the delivering of a lecture by an entire stranger on 'Cigar Ends He Has Met,' strikes me as ridiculous in the extreme. Of what earthly interest is it to us to know that this or that cigar was smoked by Captain Kidd?"

"Merely that it will help us on, your honor, to discover the whereabouts of the said Kidd," interposed the stranger. "It is by trifles, seeming trifles, that the greatest detective work is done. My friends Le Coq, Hawkshaw, and Old Sleuth will bear me out in this, I think, however much in other respects our methods may have differed. They left no stone unturned in the pursuit of a criminal; no detail, however trifling, uncared for. No more should we in the present instance overlook the minutest bit of evidence, however irrelevant and absurd at first blush it may appear to be. The truth of what I say was very effectually proven in the strange case of the Brokedale tiara, in which I figured somewhat conspicuously, but which I have never made public, because it involves a secret affecting the integrity of one of the noblest families in the British Empire. I really believe that mystery was solved easily and at once because I happened to remember that the number of my watch was 86507B. How trivial a thing, and yet how important it was, as the event transpired, you will realize when I tell you the incident."

The stranger's manner was so impressive that there was a unanimous and simultaneous movement upon the part of all present to get up closer, so as the more readily to hear what he said, as a result of which poor old Boswell was pushed overboard, and fell with a loud splash into the Styx. Fortunately, however, one of Cha-

"POOR OLD BOSWELL WAS PUSHED OVERBOARD"

ron's pleasure - boats was close at hand,
and in a short while the dripping, sputter-
ing spirit was drawn into it, wrung out,
and sent home to dry. The excitement
attending this diversion having subsided,
Solomon asked:

"What was the incident of the lost
tiara ?"

"I am about to tell you," returned the
stranger; "and it must be understood
that you are told in the strictest confidence, for, as I say, the incident involves
a state secret of great magnitude. In
life—in the mortal life—gentlemen, I was
a detective by profession, and, if I do say
it, who perhaps should not, I was one of
the most interesting for purely literary
purposes that has ever been known. I did
not find it necessary to go about saying
'Ha! ha!' as M. Le Coq was accustomed
to do to advertise his cleverness; neither
did I disguise myself as a drum-major and
hide under a kitchen-table for the purpose of solving a mystery involving the
abduction of a parlor stove, after the man-

ner of the talented Hawkshaw. By mental concentration alone, without fireworks or orchestral accompaniment of any sort whatsoever, did I go about my business, and for that very reason many of my fellow - sleuths were forced to go out of real detective work into that line of the business with which the stage has familiarized the most of us—a line in which nothing but stupidity, luck, and a yellow wig is required of him who pursues it."

"This man is an impostor," whispered Le Coq to Hawkshaw.

"I've known that all along by the mole on his left wrist," returned Hawkshaw, contemptuously.

"I suspected it the minute I saw he was not disguised," returned Le Coq, knowingly. "I have observed that the greatest villains latterly have discarded disguises, as being too easily penetrated, and therefore of no avail, and merely a useless expense."

"Silence!" cried Confucius, impatiently. "How can the gentleman proceed, with all this conversation going on in the rear ?"

Hawkshaw and Le Coq immediately subsided, and the stranger went on.

"It was in this way that I treated the strange case of the lost tiara," resumed the stranger. "Mental concentration upon seemingly insignificant details alone enabled me to bring about the desired results in that instance. A brief outline of the case is as follows: It was late one evening in the early spring of 1894. The London season was at its height. Dances, fêtes of all kinds, opera, and the theatres were in full blast, when all of a sudden society was paralyzed by a most audacious robbery. A diamond tiara valued at £50,-000 sterling had been stolen from the Duchess of Brokedale, and under circumstances which threw society itself and every individual in it under suspicion — even his Royal Highness the Prince himself, for he had danced frequently with the Duchess, and was known to be a great admirer of her tiara. It was at half-past eleven

o'clock at night that the news of the robbery first came to my ears. I had been
spending the evening alone in my library
making notes for a second volume of my
memoirs, and, feeling somewhat depressed,
I was on the point of going out for my
usual midnight walk on Hampstead Heath,
when one of my servants, hastily entering, informed me of the robbery. I
changed my mind in respect to my midnight walk immediately upon receipt of
the news, for I knew that before one
o'clock some one would call upon me at
my lodgings with reference to this robbery. It could not be otherwise. Any
mystery of such magnitude could no more
be taken to another bureau than elephants
could fly—"

"They used to," said Adam. "I once
had a whole aviary full of winged elephants. They flew from flower to flower, and thrusting their probabilities deep
into—"

"Their what?" queried Johnson, with a
frown.

"Probabilities—isn't that the word? Their trunks," said Adam.

"Probosces, I imagine you mean," suggested Johnson.

"Yes—that was it. Their probosces," said Adam. "They were great honey-gatherers, those elephants—far better than the bees, because they could make so much more of it in a given time."

Munchausen shook his head sadly. "I'm afraid I'm outclassed by these antediluvians," he said.

"Gentlemen! gentlemen!" cried Sir Walter. "These interruptions are inexcusable!"

"That's what I think," said the stranger, with some asperity. "I'm having about as hard a time getting this story out as I would if it were a serial. Of course, if you gentlemen do not wish to hear it, I can stop; but it must be understood that when I do stop I stop finally, once and for all, because the tale has not a sufficiency of dramatic climaxes to warrant its prolongation over

the usual magazine period of twelve
months."

"Go on ! go on !" cried some.

"Shut up !" cried others—addressing
the interrupting members, of course.

"As I was saying," resumed the stranger, "I felt confident that within an hour,
in some way or other, that case would be
placed in my hands. It would be mine
either positively or negatively—that is to
say, either the person robbed would em-
ploy me to ferret out the mystery and
recover the diamonds, or the robber himself, actuated by motives of self-preserva-
tion, would endeavor to direct my ener-
gies into other channels until he should
have the time to dispose of his ill-gotten
booty. A mental discussion of the probabilities inclined me to believe that the
latter would be the case. I reasoned in
this fashion : The person robbed is of ex-
alted rank. She cannot move rapidly because she is so. Great bodies move slowly. It is probable that it will be a week
before, according to the etiquette by

which she is hedged about, she can communicate with me.   In the first place, she
must inform one of her attendants that she
has been robbed.   He must communicate
the news to the functionary in charge of
her residence, who will communicate with
the Home Secretary, and from him will
issue the orders to the police, who, baffled
at every step, will finally address themselves to me.   'I'll give that side two
weeks,' I said.   On the other hand, the
robber : will he allow himself to be lulled
into a false sense of security by counting
on this delay, or will he not, noting my
habit of occasionally entering upon detective enterprises of this nature of my own
volition, come to me at once and set me
to work ferreting out some crime that has
never been committed ?   My feeling was
that this would happen, and I pulled out
my watch to see if it were not nearly time
for him to arrive.   The robbery had taken
place at a state ball at the Buckingham
Palace.   'H'm !' I mused.   'He has had
an hour and forty minutes to get here.

It is now twelve twenty. He should be
here by twelve forty-five. I will wait.'
And hastily swallowing a cocaine tablet
to nerve myself up for the meeting, I sat
down and began to read my Schopen-
hauer. Hardly had I perused a page
when there came a tap upon my door.   I
rose with a smile, for I thought I knew
what was to happen, opened the door, and
there stood, much to my surprise, the
husband of the lady whose tiara was missing.   It was the Duke of Brokedale himself.   It is true he was disguised. His
beard was powdered until it looked like
snow, and he wore a wig and a pair of
green goggles ; but I recognized him at
once by his lack of manners, which is
an unmistakable sign of nobility. As I
opened the door, he began :

" ' You are Mr.—'

" 'I am,' I replied. 'Come in. You
have come to see me about your stolen
watch. It is a gold hunting-case watch
with a Swiss movement ; loses five minutes a day ; stem-winder ; and the back

cover, which does not bear any inscription, has upon it the indentations made by the molars of your son Willie when that interesting youth was cutting his teeth upon it.'"

"Wonderful!" cried Johnson.

"May I ask how you knew all that?" asked Solomon, deeply impressed. "Such penetration strikes me as marvellous."

"I didn't know it," replied the stranger, with a smile. "What I said was intended to be jocular, and to put Brokedale at his ease. The Americans present, with their usual astuteness, would term it bluff. It was. I merely rattled on. I simply did not wish to offend the gentleman by letting him know that I had penetrated his disguise. Imagine my surprise, however, when his eye brightened as I spoke, and he entered my room with such alacrity that half the powder which he thought disguised his beard was shaken off on to the floor. Sitting down in the chair I had just vacated, he quietly remarked :

" ' You are a wonderful man, sir.   How
did you know that I had lost my watch ?'

"For a moment I was nonplussed ;
more than that, I was completely stag-
gered.   I had expected him to say at once
that he had not lost his watch, but had
come to see me about the tiara ; and to
have him take my words seriously was
entirely unexpected and overwhelmingly
surprising.   However, in view of his rank,
I deemed it well to fall in with his humor.
' Oh, as for that,' I replied, ' that is a
part of my business.   It is the detective's
place to know everything ; and generally,
if he reveals the machinery by means of
which he reaches his conclusions, he is a
fool, since his method is his secret, and
his secret his stock in trade.   I do not
mind telling you, however, that I knew
your watch was stolen by your anxious
glance at my clock, which showed that
you wished to know the time.   Now
most rich Americans have watches for
that purpose, and have no hesitation
about showing them.   If you'd had a

watch, you'd have looked at it, not at my clock.'

"My visitor laughed, and repeated what he had said about my being a wonderful man.

"'And the dents which my son made cutting his teeth?' he added.

"'Invariably go with an American's watch.   Rubber or ivory rings aren't good enough for American babies to chew on.' said I.   'They must have gold watches or nothing.'

"'And finally, how did you know I was a rich American?' he asked.

"'Because no other can afford to stop at hotels like the Savoy in the height of the season,' I replied, thinking that the jest would end there, and that he would now reveal his identity and speak of the tiara.   To my surprise, however, he did nothing of the sort.

"'You have an almost supernatural gift,' he said.   'My name is Bunker.   I *am* stopping at the Savoy.   I *am* an American.   I *was* rich when I arrived

here, but I'm not quite so bloated with
wealth as I was, now that I have paid my
first week's bill. I *have* lost my watch ;
such a watch, too, as you describe, even
to the dents.   Your only mistake was that
the dents were made by my son John, and
not Willie ; but even there I cannot but
wonder at you, for John and Willie are
twins, and so much alike that it some-
times baffles even their mother to tell
them apart.   The watch has no very great
value intrinsically, but the associations
are such that I want it back, and I will
pay £200 for its recovery.   I have no clew
as to who took it.   It was numbered—'

"Here a happy thought struck me.   In
all my description of the watch I had
merely described my own, a very cheap
affair which I had won at a raffle.   My
visitor was deceiving me, though for what
purpose I did not on the instant divine.
No one would like to suspect him of having purloined his wife's tiara.   Why
should I not deceive him, and at the same
time get rid of my poor chronometer for a

sum that exceeded its value a hundred-fold?"

"Good business!" cried Shylock.

The stranger smiled and bowed.

"Excellent," he said. "I took the words right out of his mouth. 'It was numbered 86507B!' I cried, giving, of course, the number of my own watch.

"He gazed at me narrowly for a moment, and then he smiled. 'You grow more marvellous at every step. That was indeed the number. Are you a demon?'

"'No,' I replied. 'Only something of a mind-reader.'

"Well, to be brief, the bargain was struck. I was to look for a watch that I knew he hadn't lost, and was to receive £200 if I found it. It seemed to him to be a very good bargain, as, indeed, it was, from his point of view, feeling, as he did, that there never having been any such watch, it could not be recovered, and little suspecting that two could play at his little game of deception, and that under any circumstances I could foist a ten-shilling watch upon him for two hundred pounds. This business concluded, he started to go.

"'Won't you have a little Scotch?' I asked, as he started, feeling, with all that prospective profit in view, I could well afford the expense. 'It is a stormy night.'

"'Thanks, I will,' said he, returning and seating himself by my table—still, to my surprise, keeping his hat on.

"Let me take your hat,' I said, little thinking that my courtesy would reveal the true state of affairs. The mere mention of the word hat brought about a terrible change in my visitor; his knees trembled, his face grew ghastly, and he clutched the brim of his beaver until it cracked. He then nervously removed it, and I noticed a dull red mark running about his forehead, just as there would be on the forehead of a man whose hat fitted too tightly; and that mark, gentlemen, had the undulating outline of nothing more nor less than a tiara, and on the apex of the uppermost extremity was a deep indentation about the size of a shilling, that could have been made only by some adamantine substance ! The mystery was solved ! The robber of the Duchess of Brokedale stood before me."

A suppressed murmur of excitement went through the assembled spirits, and even Messrs. Hawkshaw and Le Coq were silent in the presence of such genius.

"My plan of action was immediately formulated. The man was completely at my mercy. He had stolen the tiara, and had it concealed in the lining of his hat. I rose and locked the door. My visitor sank with a groan into my chair.

"'Why did you do that?' he stammered, as I turned the key in the lock.

"'To keep my Scotch whiskey from evaporating,' I said, dryly. 'Now, my lord,' I added, 'it will pay your Grace to let me have your hat. I know who you are. You are the Duke of Brokedale. The Duchess of Brokedale has lost a valuable tiara of diamonds, and you have not

lost your watch. Somebody has stolen
the diamonds, and it may be that somewhere there is a Bunker who has lost such
a watch as I have described. The queer
part of it all is,' I continued, handing him
the decanter, and taking a couple of loaded six-shooters out of my escritoire—'the
queer part of it all is that I have the
watch and you have the tiara. We'll swap
the swag. Hand over the bauble, please.'

"'But—' he began.

"'We won't have any butting, your
Grace,' said I.   'I'll give you the watch,
and you needn't mind the £200 ; and you
must give me the tiara, or I'll accompany
you forthwith to the police, and have a
search made of your hat. It won't pay
you to defy me. Give it up.'

"He gave up the hat at once, and, as I
suspected, there lay the tiara, snugly
stowed away behind the head-band.

"'You are a great fellow.' said I, as I
held the tiara up to the light and watched
with pleasure the flashing brilliance of its
gems.

"'I beg you'll not expose me,' he moaned. 'I was driven to it by necessity.'

"'Not I,' I replied. 'As long as you play fair it will be all right. I'm not going to keep this thing. I'm not married, and so have no use for such a trifle; but what I do intend is simply to wait until your wife retains me to find it, and then I'll find it and get the reward. If you keep perfectly still, I'll have it found in such a fashion that you'll never be suspected. If, on the other hand, you say a word about to-night's events, I'll hand you over to the police.'

"'Humph!' he said. 'You couldn't prove a case against me.'

"'I can prove any case against anybody,' I retorted. 'If you don't believe it, read my book,' I added, and I handed him a copy of my memoirs.

"'I've read it,' he answered, 'and I ought to have known better than to come here. I thought you were only a literary success.' And with a deep-drawn sigh he took the watch and went out. Ten days later I was retained by the Duchess, and after a pretended search of ten days more I found the tiara, restored it to the noble lady, and received the £5000 reward. The Duke kept perfectly quiet about our little encounter, and afterwards we became stanch friends; for he was a good fellow, and was driven to his desperate deed only by the demands of his creditors, and the following Christmas he sent me the watch I had given him, with the best wishes of the season.

"So, you see, gentlemen, in a moment, by quick wit and a mental concentration of no mean order, combined with strict observance of the pettiest details, I ferreted out what bade fair to become a great diamond mystery; and when I say that this cigar end proves certain things to my mind, it does not become you to doubt the value of my conclusions."

"Hear! hear!" cried Raleigh, growing tumultuous with enthusiasm.

"Your name? your name?" came from all parts of the wharf.

The stranger, putting his hand into the folds of his coat, drew forth a bundle of business cards, which he tossed, as the prestidigitator tosses playing-cards, out among the audience, and on each of them was found printed the words :

SHERLOCK HOLMES,

DETECTIVE.

———

FERRETING DONE HERE.

———

Plots for Sale.

"I think he made a mistake in not taking the £200 for the watch. Such carelessness destroys my confidence in him," said Shylock, who was the first to recover from the surprise of the revelation.

III

THE SEARCH-PARTY IS ORGANIZED

"WELL, Mr. Holmes," said Sir Walter
Raleigh, after three rousing cheers, led by
Hamlet, had been given with a will by the
assembled spirits, "after this demonstration in your honor I think it is hardly
necessary for me to assure you of our
hearty co-operation in anything you may
venture to suggest. There is still manifest, however, some desire on the part of
the ever-wise King Solomon and my
friend Confucius to know how you deduce
that Kidd has sailed for London, from the
cigar end which you hold in your hand."

"I can easily satisfy their curiosity,"
said Sherlock Holmes, genially. "I believe I have already proven that it is the
end of Kidd's cigar. The marks of the

"THREE ROUSING CHEERS, LED BY HAMLET, WERE GIVEN"

teeth have shown that. Now observe how
closely it is smoked — there is barely
enough of it left for one to insert between
his teeth. Now Captain Kidd would
hardly have risked the edges of his mus-
tache and the comfort of his lips by smok-
ing a cigar down to the very light if he
had had another ; nor would he under any
circumstances have smoked it that far unless he were passionately addicted to this
particular brand of the weed. Therefore
I say to you, first, this was his cigar ;
second, it was the last one he had ; third,
he is a confirmed smoker. The result, he
has gone to the one place in the world
where these Connecticut hand-rolled Havana cigars—for I recognize this as one of
them — have a real popularity, and are
therefore more certainly obtainable, and
that is at London. You cannot get so
vile a cigar as that outside of a London
hotel. If I could have seen a quarter-
inch more of it, I should have been able
definitely to locate the hotel itself. The
wrappers unroll to a degree that varies

perceptibly as between the different hotels. The Metropole cigar can be smoked
a quarter through before its wrapper gives
way; the Grand wrapper goes as soon as
you light the cigar; whereas the Savoy,
fronting on the Thames, is surrounded by
a moister atmosphere than the others, and,
as a consequence, the wrapper will hold
really until most people are willing to
throw the whole thing away."

"It is really a wonderful art!" said
Solomon.

"The making of a Connecticut Havana
cigar?" laughed Holmes. "Not at all.
Give me a head of lettuce and a straw,
and I'll make you a box."

"I referred to your art — that of de-
tection," said Solomon. "Your logic is
perfect; step by step we have been led to
the irresistible conclusion that Kidd has
made for London, and can be found at
one of these hotels."

"And only until next Tuesday, when
he will take a house in the neighborhood
of Scotland Yard," put in Holmes, quick-

ly, observing a sneer on Hawkshaw's lips, and hastening to overwhelm him by further evidence of his ingenuity. "When he gets his bill he will open his piratical eyes so wide that he will be seized with jealousy to think of how much more refined his profession has become since he left it, and out of mere pique he will leave the hotel, and, to show himself still cleverer than his modern prototypes, he will leave his account unpaid, with the result that the affair will be put in the hands of the police, under which circumstances a house in the immediate vicinity of the famous police headquarters will be the safest hiding-place he can find, as was instanced by the remarkable case of the famous Penstock bond robbery. A certain church-warden named Hinkley, having been appointed cashier thereof, robbed the Penstock Imperial Bank of £1,000,-000 in bonds, and, fleeing to London, actually joined the detective force at Scotland Yard, and was detailed to find himself, which of course he never did, nor would he ever have been found had he not crossed my path."

Hawkshaw gazed mournfully off into space, and Le Coq muttered profane words under his breath.

"We're not in the same class with this fellow, Hawkshaw," said Le Coq. "You could tap your forehead knowingly eight hours a day through all eternity with a sledge-hammer without loosening an idea like that."

"Nevertheless I'll confound him yet," growled the jealous detective. "I shall myself go to London, and, disguised as Captain Kidd, will lead this visionary on until he comes there to arrest me, and when these club members discover that it is Hawkshaw and not Kidd he has run to earth, we'll have a great laugh on Sherlock Holmes."

"I am anxious to hear how you solved the bond-robbery mystery," said Socrates, wrapping his toga closely about him and settling back against one of the spiles of the wharf.

"So are we all," said Sir Walter. "But meantime the House-boat is getting farther away."

"Not unless she's sailing backwards," sneered Noah, who was still nursing his resentment against Sir Christopher Wren for his reflections upon the speed of the Ark.

"What's the hurry?" asked Socrates. "I believe in making haste slowly; and on the admission of our two eminent naval architects, Sir Christopher and Noah, neither of their vessels can travel more than a mile a week, and if we charter the *Flying Dutchman* to go in pursuit of her we can catch her before she gets out of the Styx into the Atlantic."

"Jonah might lend us his whale, if the beast is in commission," suggested Munchausen, dryly. "I for one would rather take a state-room in Jonah's whale than go aboard the *Flying Dutchman* again. I made one trip on the *Dutchman*, and she's worse than a dory for comfort; furthermore, I don't see what good it would do us to charter a boat that can't land oftener than once in seven years, and spends most of her time trying to double the Cape of Good Hope."

"My whale is in commission," said Jonah, with dignity. " But Baron Munchausen need not consider the question of taking a state-room aboard of her. She doesn't carry second - class passengers. And if I took any stock in the idea of a trip on the *Flying Dutchman* amounting to a seven years' exile, I would cheerfully pay the Baron's expenses for a round trip."

" We are losing time, gentlemen," suggested Sherlock Holmes. " This is a moment, I think, when you should lay aside personal differences and personal preferences for immediate action. I have examined the wake of the House-boat, and I judge from the condition of what, for want of a better term, I may call the suds, when she left us the House-boat was making ten knots a day. Almost any craft we can find suitably manned ought to be able to do better than that; and if you could summon Charon and ascertain what boats he has at hand, it would be for the good of all concerned."

"That's a good plan," said Johnson. "Boswell, see if you can find Charon."

"I am here already, sir," returned the ferryman, rising. "Most of my boats have gone into winter quarters, your Honor. The *Mayflower* went into dry dock last week to be calked up; the *Pinta* and the *Santa Maria* are slow and cranky; the *Monitor* and the *Merrimac* I haven't really had time to patch up; and the *Valkyrie* is two months overdue. I cannot make up my mind whether she is lost or kept back by excursion steamers. Hence I really don't know what I can lend you. Any of these boats I have named you could have had for nothing; but my others are actively employed, and I couldn't let them go without a serious interference with my business."

The old man blinked sorrowfully across the waters at the opposite shore. It was

4

quite evident that he realized what a
dreadful expense the club was about to be
put to, and while of course there would be
profit in it for him, he was sincerely sorry
for them.

"I repeat," he added, "those boats you
could have had for nothing, but the others I'd have to charge you for, though of
course I'll give you a discount."

And he blinked again, as he meditated
upon whether that discount should be an
eighth or one-quarter of one per cent.

"The *Flying Dutchman*," he pursued,
"ain't no good for your purposes. She's
too fast. She's built to fly by, not to
stop. You'd catch up with the House-
boat in a minute with her, but you'd go
right on and disappear like a visionary;
and as for the Ark, she'd never do—with
all respect to Mr. Noah. She's just about
as suitable as any other waterlogged cat-
tle-steamer 'd be, and no more—first-rate
for elephants and kangaroos, but no good
for cruiser-work, and so slow she wouldn't
make a ripple high enough to drown a

gnat going at the top of her speed.   Furthermore, she's got a great big hole in her
bottom, where she was stove in by running afoul of—Mount Arrus-root, I believe
it was called when Captain Noah went
cruising with that menagerie of his."

"That's an unmitigated falsehood!"
cried Noah, angrily.   "This man talks
like a professional amateur yachtsman.
He has no regard for facts, but simply
goes ahead and makes statements with an
utter disregard of the truth.   The Ark
was not stove in.   We beached her very
successfully.   I say this in defence of my
seamanship, which was top-notch for my
day."

"Couldn't sail six weeks without foul-
ing a mountain - peak!" sneered Wren,
perceiving a chance to get even.

"The hole's there, just the same," said
Charon.   "Maybe she was a centreboard,
and that's where you kept the board."

"The hole is there because it was worn
there by one of the elephants," retorted
Noah.   "You get a beast like the ele-

phant shuffling one of his fore-feet up and down, up and down, a plank for twenty-four hours a day for forty days in one of your boats, and see where your boat would be."

"Thanks," said Charon, calmly. "But the elephants don't patronize my line. All the elephants I've ever seen in Hades waded over, except Jumbo, and he reached his trunk across, fastened on to a tree limb with it, and swung himself over. However, the Ark isn't at all what you want, unless you are going to man her with a lot of centaurs. If that's your intention, I'd charter her; the accommodations are just the thing for a crew of that kind."

"Well, what do you suggest?" asked Raleigh, somewhat impatiently. "You've told us what we can't do. Now tell us what we can do."

"I'd stay right here," said Charon, "and let the ladies rescue themselves. That's what I'd do. I've had the honor of bringing 'em over here, and I think I know 'em pretty well.   I've watched 'em close, and it's my private opinion that before many days you'll see your club-house sailing back here, with Queen Elizabeth at the hellum, and the other ladies on the for'ard deck knittin' and crochetin', and tearin' each other to pieces in a conversational way, as happy as if there never had been any Captain Kidd and his pirate crew."

"That suggestion is impossible," said Blackstone, rising.   "Whether the relief expedition amounts to anything or not, it's good to be set going.   The ladies would never forgive us if we sat here inactive, even if they were capable of rescuing themselves.   It is an accepted principle of law that this climate hath no fury like a woman left to herself, and we've got enough professional furies hereabouts without our aiding in augmenting the ranks.   We must have a boat."

"It'll cost you a thousand dollars a week," said Charon.

"I'll subscribe fifty," cried Hamlet.

"I'll consult my secretary," said Solomon, "and find out how many of my wives have been abducted, and I'll pay ten dollars apiece for their recovery."

"That's liberal," said Hawkshaw. "There are sixty-three of 'em on board, together with eighty of his fiancées. What's the quotation on fiancées, King Solomon?"

"Nothing," said Solomon. "They're not mine yet, and it's their fathers' business to get 'em back. Not mine."

Other subscriptions came pouring in, and it was not long before everybody save Shylock had put his name down for something. This some one of the more quick-witted of the spirits soon observed, and, with reckless disregard of the feelings of the Merchant of Venice, began to call: "Shylock! Shylock! How much?"

The Merchant tried to leave the pier, but his path was blocked.

"Subscribe, subscribe!" was the cry. "How much?"

"Order, gentlemen, order!" said Sir

A BLACK PERSON BY THE NAME OF FRIDAY FINDS A BOTTLE

Walter, rising and holding a bottle aloft. "A black person by the name of Friday, a valet of our friend Mr. Crusoe, has just handed me this bottle, which he picked up ten minutes ago on the bank of the river a few miles distant. It contains a bit of paper, and may perhaps give us a clew based upon something more substantial than even the wonderful theories of our new brother Holmes."

A deathly silence followed the chairman's words, as Sir Walter drew a corkscrew from his pocket and opened the bottle. He extracted the paper, and, as he had surmised, it proved to be a message from the missing vessel. His face brightening with a smile of relief, Sir Walter read, aloud :

"Have just emerged into the Atlantic. Club in hands of Kidd and forty ruffians. One hundred and eighty-three ladies on board. Headed for the Azores. Send aid at once. All well except Xanthippe, who is seasick in the billiard-room. (Signed) Portia."

"Aha !" cried Hawkshaw.   "That shows how valuable the Holmes theory is."

"Precisely," said Holmes.   "No woman knows anything about seafaring, but Portia is right.   The ship is headed for the Azores, which is the first tack needed in a windward sail for London under the present conditions."

The reply was greeted with cheers, and when they subsided the cry for Shylock's subscription began again, but he declined.

"I had intended to put up a thousand ducats," he said, defiantly, "but with that woman Portia on board I won't give a red obolus !" and with that he wrapped his cloak about him and stalked off into the gathering shadows of the wood.

And so the funds were raised without the aid of Shylock, and the shapely twin-screw steamer the *Gehenna* was chartered of Charon, and put under the command of Mr. Sherlock Holmes, who, after he had thanked the company for their confidence, walked abstractedly away, observing in strictest confidence to himself that he had done well to prepare that bottle beforehand and bribe Crusoe's man to find it.

"For now," he said, with a chuckle, "I can get back to earth again free of cost on my own hook, whether my eminent inventor wants me there or not. I never approved of his killing me off as he did at the very height of my popularity."

IV

ON BOARD THE HOUSE-BOAT

MEANWHILE the ladies were not having such a bad time, after all. Once having gained possession of the House-boat, they were loath to think of ever having to give it up again, and it is an open question in my mind if they would not have made off with it themselves had Captain Kidd and his men not done it for them.

"I'll never forgive these men for their selfishness in monopolizing all this," said Elizabeth, with a vicious stroke of a billiard-cue, which missed the cue-ball and tore a right angle in the cloth. "It is not right."

"No," said Portia. "It is all wrong; and when we get back home I'm going to give my beloved Bassanio a piece of my mind; and if he doesn't give in to me,

I'll reverse my decision in the famous case of Shylock *versus* Antonio."

"Then I sincerely hope he doesn't give in," retorted Cleopatra, "for I swear by all my auburn locks that that was the very worst bit of injustice ever perpetrated. Mr. Shakespeare confided to me one night, at one of Mrs. Cæsar's card-parties, that he regarded that as the biggest joke he ever wrote, and Judge Blackstone observed to Antony that the decision wouldn't have held in any court of equity outside of Venice. If you owe a man a thousand ducats, and it costs you three thousand to get them, that's your affair, not his. If it cost Antonio every drop of his bluest blood to pay the pound of flesh, it was Antonio's affair, not Shylock's. However, the world applauds you as a great jurist, when you have nothing more than a woman's keen instinct for sentimental technicalities."

"It would have made a horrid play, though, if it had gone on," shuddered Elizabeth.

"That may be, but, carried out realistically, it would have done away with a raft of bad actors," said Cleopatra. " I'm half sorry it didn't go on, and I'm sure it wouldn't have been any worse than compelling Brutus to fall on his sword until he resembles a chicken liver *en brochette,* as is done in that Julius Cæsar play."

"Well, I'm very glad I did it," snapped Portia.

"I should think you would be," said Cleopatra. "If you hadn't done it, you'd never have been known. What was that ?"

The boat had given a slight lurch.

"Didn't you hear a shuffling noise up on deck, Portia ?" asked the Egyptian Queen.

"I thought I did, and it seemed as if the vessel had moved a bit," returned Portia, nervously ; for, like most women in an advanced state of development, she had become a martyr to her nerves.

"It was merely the wash from one of Charon's new ferry-boats, I fancy," said Elizabeth, calmly. " It's disgusting, the way that old fellow allows these modern innovations to be brought in here ! As if the old paddle-boats he used to carry shades in weren't good enough for the immigrants of this age! Really this Styx River is losing a great deal of its charm. Sir Walter and I were upset, while out rowing one day last summer, by the waves kicked up by one of Charon's excursion steamers going up the river with a party of picnickers from the city — the Greater Gehenna Chowder Club, I believe it was —on board of her. One might just as well live in the midst of the turmoil of a great city as try to get uninterrupted quiet here in the suburbs in these days. Charon isn't content to get rich slowly; he must make money by the barrelful, if he has to sacrifice all the comfort of everybody living on this river. Anybody 'd think he was an American, the way he goes on; and everybody else here is the same way. The Erebeans are getting to be a race of shopkeepers."

"I think myself," sighed Cleopatra, "that Hades is being spoiled by the introduction of American ideas—it is get-

ting by far too democratic for my tastes;
and if it isn't stopped, it's my belief that
the best people will stop coming here.
Take Madame Récamier's salon as it is
now and compare it with what it used to
be! In the early days, after her arrival
here, everybody went because it was the
swell thing, and you'd be sure of meeting
the intellectually elect. On the one hand
you'd find Sophocles; on the other,
Cicero; across the room would be Horace
chatting gayly with some such person as
myself. Great warriors, from Alexander
to Bonaparte, were there, and glad of the
opportunity to be there, too; statesmen
like Macchiavelli; artists like Cellini or
Tintoretto. You couldn't move without
stepping on the toes of genius. But now
all is different. The money-getting instinct has been aroused within them all,
with the result that when I invited Mozart
to meet a few friends at dinner at my
place last autumn, he sent me a card stating his terms for dinners. Let me see, I
think I have it with me; I've kept it by
me for fear of losing it, it is such a com-

plete revelation of the actual condition of
affairs in this locality. Ah! this is it,"
she added, taking a small bit of paste-
board from her card-case. "Read that."

The card was passed about, and all the
ladies were much astonished—and natu-
rally so, for it ran this wise:

NOTICE TO HOSTESSES.

Owing to the very great, constantly growing, and at times vexatious demands upon
his time socially,

HERR WOLFGANG AMADEUS MOZART

takes this method of announcing to his
friends that on and after January 1, 1897,
his terms for functions will be as follows:

	Marks.
Dinners with conversation on the Theory of Music............	500
Dinners with conversation on the Theory of Music, illustrated...	750
Dinners without any conversation......................	300
Receptions, public, with music...	1000
" private, " ...	750
Encores (single)...............	100
Three encores for	150
Autographs...................	10

Positively no Invitations for Five-o'Clock
Teas or Morning Musicales considered.

"Well, I declare!" tittered Elizabeth, as she read. "Isn't that extraordinary? He's got the three-name craze, too!"

"It's perfectly ridiculous," said Cleopatra. "But it's fairer than Artemus Ward's plan. Mozart gives notice of his intentions to charge you; but with Ward it's different. He comes, and afterwards sends a bill for his fun. Why, only last week I got a 'quarterly statement' from him showing a charge against me of thirty-eight dollars for humorous remarks made to my guests at a little chafing-dish party I gave in honor of Balzac, and, worst of all, he had marked it 'Please remit.' Even Antony, when he wrote a sonnet to my eyebrow, wouldn't let me have it until he had heard whether or not Boswell wanted it for publication in the *Gossip*. With Rubens giving chalk-talks for pay, Phidias doing 'Five-minute Masterpieces in Putty' for suburban lyceums, and all the illustrious in other lines turning their genius to account through the entertainment bureaus, it's impossible to have a salon now."

"You are indeed right," said Madame Récamier, sadly. "Those were palmy days when genius was satisfied with chicken salad and lemonade. I shall never forget those nights when the wit and wisdom of all time were—ah—were on tap at my house, if I may so speak, at a cost to me of lights and supper. Now the only people who will come for nothing are those we used to think of paying to stay away. Boswell is always ready, but you can't run a salon on Boswell."

"Well," said Portia, "I sincerely hope that you won't give up the functions altogether, because I have always found them most delightful. It is still possible to have lights and supper."

"I have a plan for next winter," said Madame Récamier, "but I suppose I shall be accused of going into the commercial side of it if I adopt it. The plan is, briefly, to incorporate my salon. That's an idea worthy of an American, I admit;

5

but if I don't do it I'll have to give it up entirely, which, as you intimate, would be too bad. An incorporated salon, however, would be a grand thing, if only because it would perpetuate the salon. 'The Ré-camier Salon (Limited)' would be a most excellent title, and, suitably capitalized, would enable us to pay our lions suffi-ciently. Private enterprise is powerless under modern conditions. It's as much as I can afford to pay for a dinner, with-out running up an expense account for guests; and unless we get up a salon trust, as it were, the whole affair must go to the wall."

"How would you make it pay?" asked Portia. "I can't see where your divi-dends would come from."

"That is simple enough," said Madame Récamier. "We could put up a large reception-hall with a portion of our capi-tal, and advertise a series of nights — say one a week throughout the season. These would be Warriors' Night, Story-tellers' Night, Poets' Night, Chafing-dish

MADAME RÉCAMIER HAS A PLAN

Night under the charge of Brillat - Sava-rin, and so on. It would be understood that on these particular evenings the most interesting people in certain lines would be present, and would mix with outsiders, who should be admitted only on payment of a certain sum of money. The commonplace inhabitants of this country could thus meet the truly great; and if I know them well, as I think I do, they'll pay readily for the privilege. The obscure love to rub up against the famous here as well as they do on earth."

"You'd run a sort of Social Zoo?" suggested Elizabeth.

"Precisely; and provide entertainment for private residences too. An advertisement in Boswell's paper, which everybody buys—"

"And which nobody reads," said Portia.

"They read the advertisements," retorted Madame Récamier. "As I was saying, an advertisement could be placed in Boswell's paper as follows : ' Are you

giving a Function ? Do you want Talent?
Get your Genius at the Récamier Salon
(Limited).' It would be simply magnifi-
cent as a business enterprise. The com-
mon herd would be tickled to death if
they could get great people at their
homes, even if they had to pay roundly
for them."

"It would look well in the society
notes, wouldn't it, if Mr. John Boggs
gave a reception, and at the close of the
account it said, ' The supper was fur-
nished by Calizetti, and the genius by the
Récamier Salon (Limited)' ?" suggested
Elizabeth, scornfully.

"I must admit," replied the French
lady, "that you call up an unpleasant
possibility, but I don't really see what
else we can do if we want to preserve the
salon idea. Somebody has told these
talented people that they have a commercial value, and they are availing themselves of the demand."

"It is a sad age !" sighed Elizabeth.

"Well, all I've got to say is just this,"

put in Xanthippe : "You people who get up functions have brought this condition of affairs on yourselves. You were not satisfied to go ahead and indulge your passion for lions in a moderate fashion. Take the case of Demosthenes last winter, for instance. His wife told me that he dined at home three times during the winter. The rest of the time he was out, here, there, and everywhere, making after-dinner speeches. The saving on his dinner bills didn't pay his pebble account, much less remunerate him for his time, and the fearful expense of nervous energy to which he was subjected. It was as much as she could do, she said, to keep him from shaving one side of his head, so that he couldn't go out, the way he used to do in Athens when he was afraid he would be invited out and couldn't scare up a decent excuse for refusing."

"Did he do that ?" cried Elizabeth, with a roar of laughter.

"So the cyclopædias say. It's a good

plan, too," said Xanthippe. "Though Socrates never had to do it. When I got the notion Socrates was going out too much, I used to hide his dress clothes. Then there was the case of Rubens. He gave a Carbon Talk at the Sforza's Thursday Night Club, merely to oblige Madame Sforza, and three weeks later discovered that she had sold his pictures to pay for her gown! You people simply run it into the ground. You kill the goose that when taken at the flood leads on to fortune. It advertises you, does the lion no good, and he is expected to be satisfied with confectionery, material and theoretical. If they are getting tired of candy and compliments, it's because you have forced too much of it upon them."

"They like it, just the same," retorted Récamier. "A genius likes nothing better than the sound of his own voice, when he feels that it is falling on aristocratic ears. The social laurel rests pleasantly on many a noble brow."

"True," said Xanthippe. "But when

"THE HARD FEATURES OF KIDD WERE THRUST THROUGH"

a man gets a pile of Christmas wreaths a
mile high on his head, he begins to wonder what they will bring on the market.
An occasional wreath is very nice, but by
the ton they are apt to weigh on his mind.
Up to a certain point notoriety is like a
woman, and a man is apt to love it; but
when it becomes exacting, demanding instead of permitting itself to be courted, it
loses its charm."

"That is Socratic in its wisdom," smiled
Portia.

"But Xanthippic in its origin," returned Xanthippe. "No man ever gave me
my ideas."

As Xanthippe spoke, Lucretia Borgia
burst into the room.

"Hurry and save yourselves!" she cried.
"The boat has broken loose from her
moorings, and is floating down the stream.
If we don't hurry up and do something,
we'll drift out to sea!"

"What!" cried Cleopatra, dropping
her cue in terror, and rushing for the
stairs. "I was certain I felt a slight

motion. You said it was the wash from one of Charon's barges, Elizabeth."

"I thought it was," said Elizabeth, following closely after.

"Well, it wasn't," moaned Lucretia Borgia. "Calpurnia just looked out of the window and discovered that we were in mid-stream."

The ladies crowded anxiously about the stair and attempted to ascend, Cleopatra in the van; but as the Egyptian Queen reached the doorway to the upper deck, the door opened, and the hard features of Captain Kidd were thrust roughly through, and his strident voice rang out through the gathering gloom. "Pipe my eye for a sardine if we haven't captured a female seminary!" he cried.

And one by one the ladies, in terror, shrank back into the billiard-room, while Kidd, overcome by surprise, slammed the door to, and retreated into the darkness of the forward deck to consult with his followers as to "what next."

V

A CONFERENCE ON DECK

"HERE'S a kettle of fish!" said Kidd, pulling his chin whisker in perplexity as he and his fellow-pirates gathered about the capstan to discuss the situation. "I'm blessed if in all my experience I ever sailed athwart anything like it afore! Pirating with a lot of low-down ruffians like you gentlemen is bad enough, but on a craft loaded to the water's edge with advanced women— I've half a mind to turn back."

"If you do, you swim—we'll not turn back with you," retorted Abeuchapeta, whom, in honor of his prowess, Kidd had appointed executive officer of the House-boat. "I have no desire to be mutinous, Captain Kidd, but I have not embarked upon this enterprise for a pleasure sail down the Styx. I am out for business. If you had thirty thousand women on board, still should I not turn back."

"But what shall we do with 'em?" pleaded Kidd. "Where can we go without attracting attention? Who's going to feed 'em? Who's going to dress 'em? Who's going to keep 'em in bonnets? You don't know anything about these creatures, my dear Abeuchapeta; and, by-the-way, can't we arbitrate that name of yours? It would be fearful to remember in the excitement of a fight."

"Call him Ab," suggested Sir Henry Morgan, with an ill-concealed sneer, for he was deeply jealous of Abeuchapeta's preferral.

"If you do I'll call you Morgue, and change your appearance to fit," retorted Abeuchapeta, angrily.

"By the beards of all my sainted Buc- caneers," began Morgan, springing angrily to his feet, "I'll have your life!"

"Gentlemen! Gentlemen — my noble ruffians!" expostulated Kidd. "Come,

" ' HERE'S A KETTLE OF FISH,' SAID KIDD "

come ; this will never do! I must have
no quarrelling among my aides. This is
no time for divisions in our councils. An
entirely unexpected element has entered
into our affairs, and it behooveth us to
act in concert. It is no light matter—"

"Excuse me, captain," said Abeuchapeta, "but that is where you and I do not
agree. We've got our ship and we've got
our crew, and in addition we find that
the Fates have thrown in a hundred or
more women to act as ballast. Now I, for
one, do not fear a woman. We can set
them to work. There is plenty for them
to do keeping things tidy ; and if we get
into a very hard fight, and come out of
the mêlée somewhat the worse for wear,
it will be a blessing to have 'em along to
mend our togas, sew buttons on our uni-
forms, and darn our hosiery."

Morgan laughed sarcastically. "When
did you flourish, if ever, colonel?" he
asked.

"Do you refer to me?" queried Abeuchapeta, with a frown.

"You have guessed correctly," replied
Morgan, icily. "I have quite forgotten
your date ; were you a success in the year
one, or when ?"

"Admiral Abeuchapeta, Sir Henry,"
interposed Kidd, fearing a further out-
break of hostilities—"Admiral Abeuchapeta was the terror of the seas in the
seventh century, and what he undertook
to do he did, and his piratical enterprises
were carried on on a scale of magnificence
which is without parallel off the comic-
opera stage.   He never went forth without at least seventy galleys and a hundred
other vessels."

Abeuchapeta drew himself up proudly.

"Six-ninety-eight was my great year,"
he said.

"That's what I thought," said Morgan.
"That is to say, you got your ideas of
women twelve hundred years ago, and the
ladies have changed somewhat since that
time.   I have great respect for you, sir,
as a ruffian.   I have no doubt that as a
ruffian you are a complete success, but

when it comes to 'feminology' you are
sailing in unknown waters. The study of
women, my dear Abeuchadnezzar—"

"Peta," retorted Abeuchapeta, irritably.

"I stand corrected. The study of
women, my dear Peter," said Morgan,
with a wink at Conrad, which fortunately the seventh-century pirate did not see,
else there would have been an open break
—"the study of women is more difficult
than that of astronomy; there may be two
stars alike, but all women are unique.
Because she was this, that, or the other
thing in your day does not prove that she
is any one of those things in our day—in
fact, it proves the contrary. Why, I venture even to say that no individual woman is alike."

"That's rather a hazy thought," said
Kidd, scratching his head in a puzzled
sort of way.

"I mean that she's different from herself at different times," said Morgan.
"What is it the poet called her?—'an

infinite variety show,' or something of
that sort ; a perpetual vaudeville—a con-
tinuous performance, as it were, from
twelve to twelve."

"Morgan is right, admiral!" put in
Conrad the corsair, acting temporarily as
bo'sun. "The times are sadly changed,
and woman is no longer what she was.
She is hardly what she is, much less what
she was. The Roman Gynæceum would
be an impossibility to-day. You might as
well expect Delilah to open a barber-shop
on board this boat as ask any of these
advanced females below-stairs to sew buttons on a pirate's uniform after a fray, or
to keep the fringe on his epaulets curled.
They're no longer sewing-machines—they
are Keeley motors for mystery and perpetual motion. Women have views now
—they are no longer content to be looked
at merely ; they must see for themselves ;
and the more they see, the more they wish
to domesticate man and emancipate woman. It's my private opinion that if we
are to get along with them at all the best

thing to do is to let 'em alone. I have always found I was better off in the abstract,
and if this question is going to be settled
in a purely democratic fashion by submit-
ting it to a vote, I'll vote for any measure
which involves leaving them strictly to
themselves. They're nothing but a lot of
ghosts anyhow, like ourselves, and we
can pretend we don't see them."

"If that could be, it would be excellent," said Morgan ; "but it is impossible. For a pirate of the Byronic order,
my dear Conrad, you are strangely un-
versed in the ways of the sex which cheers
but not inebriates. We can no more ignore their presence upon this boat than
we can expect whales to spout kerosene.
In the first place, it would be excessively
impolite of us to cut them—to decline to
speak to them if they should address us.
We may be pirates, ruffians, cutthroats,
but I hope we shall never forget that **we**
are gentlemen."

"The whole situation is rather contrary to etiquette, don't you think ?" sug-

gested Conrad. "There's nobody to introduce us, and I can't really see how we
can do otherwise than ignore them. I
certainly am not going to stand on deck
and make eyes at them, to try and pick
up an acquaintance with them, even if I
am of a Byronic strain."

"You forget," said Kidd, "two essential features of the situation. These
women are at present — or shortly will
be, when they realize their situation—
in distress, and a true gentleman may
always fly to the rescue of a distressed
female; and, the second point, we shall
soon be on the seas, and I understand
that on the fashionable transatlantic lines
it is now considered *de rigueur* to speak
to anybody you choose to. The introduction business isn't going to stand in
my way."

"Well, may I ask," put in Abeuchapeta,
"just what it is that is worrying you ?
You said something about feeding them,
and dressing them, and keeping them in
bonnets. I fancy there's fish enough in

the sea to feed 'em; and as for their
gowns and hats, they can make 'em themselves.   Every woman is a milliner at
heart."

"Exactly, and we'll have to pay the
milliners.   That is what bothers me.   I
was going to lead this expedition to
London, Paris, and New York, admiral.
That is where the money is, and to get it
you've got to go ashore, to headquarters.
You cannot nowadays find it on the high
seas.   Modern civilization," said Kidd,
"has ruined the pirate's business.   The
latest news from the other world has
really opened my eyes to certain facts
that I never dreamed of.   The conditions
of the day of which I speak are interest-
ingly shown in the experience of our
friend Hawkins here.   Captain Hawkins,
would you have any objection to stating
to these gentlemen the condition of affairs
which led you to give up piracy on the
high seas ?"

"Not the slightest, Captain Kidd," returned Captain Hawkins, who was a re-
6

cent arrival in Hades. "It is a sad little story, and it gives me a pain for to think on it, but none the less I'll tell it, since you ask me. When I were a mere boy, fellow-pirates, I had but one ambition, due to my readin', which was confined to stories of a Sunday-school nater—to become somethin' different from the little Willies an' the clever Tommies what I read about therein. They was all good, an' they went to their reward too soon in life for me, who even in them days regarded death as a stuffy an' unpleasant diversion.   Learnin' at an early period that virtue was its only reward, an' a-wishin' others, I says to myself : 'Jim,' says I, 'if you wishes to become a magnet in this village, be sinful. If so be as you are a good boy, an' kind to your sister an' all other animals, you'll end up as a prosperous father with fifteen hundred a year sure, with never no hope for no public preferment beyond bein' made the superintendent of the Sunday-school ; but if so be as how you're bad, you may become

famous, an' go to Congress, an' have your
picture in the Sunday noospapers.' So I
looks around for books tellin' how to get
'Famous in Fifty Ways,' an' after due re-
flection I settles in my mind that to be a
pirate's just the thing for me, seein' as
how it's both profitable an' healthy. Pass-
in' over details, let me tell you that I became a pirate. I ran away to sea, an' by
dint of perseverance, as the Sunday-school
books useter say, in my badness I soon became the centre of a evil lot; an' when I
says to 'em, 'Boys, I wants to be a pirate
chief,' they hollers back, loud like, 'Jim,
we're with you,' an' they was. For years
I was the terror of the Venezuelan Gulf,
the Spanish Main, an' the Pacific seas, but
there was precious little money into it.
The best pay I got was from a Sunday
noospaper, which paid me well to sign an
article on 'Modern Piracy' which I didn't
write. Finally business got so bad the
crew began to murmur, an' I was at my
wits' ends to please 'em; when one morn-
in', havin' passed a restless night, I picks

up a noospaper and sees in it that 'Next Saturday's steamer is a weritable treasure-ship, takin' out twelve million dollars, and the jewels of a certain prima donna valued at five hundred thousand.' 'Here's my chance,' says I, an' I goes to sea and lies in wait for the steamer. I captures her easy, my crew bein' hungry, an' fightin' according like. We steals the box a-hold-in' the jewels an' the bag containin' the millions, hustles back to our own ship, an' makes for our rondyvoo, me with two bullets in my leg, four o' my crew killed, and one engin' of my ship disabled by a shot—but happy. Twelve an' a half mill-ions at one break is enough to make any-body happy."

"I should say so," said Abeuchapeta, with an ecstatic shake of his head. "I didn't get that in all my career."

"Nor I," sighed Kidd. "But go on, Hawkins."

"Well, as I says," continued Captain Hawkins, "we goes to the rondyvoo to look over our booty. 'Captain 'Awkins,'

"'EVERY BLOOMIN' MILLION WAS REPRESENTED BY A CERTIFIED CHECK, AN' PAYABLE IN LONDON'"

says my valet—for I was a swell pirate, gents, an' never travelled nowhere without a man to keep my clothes brushed and the proper wrinkles in my trousers—'this 'ere twelve millions,' says he, 'is werry light,' says he, carryin' the bag ashore.   'I don't care how light it is, so long as it's twelve millions, Henderson,' says I; but my heart sinks inside o' me at his words, an' the minute we lands I sits down to investigate right there on the beach.   I opens the bag, an' it's the one I was after —but the twelve millions!"

" Weren't there ?" cried Conrad.

"Yes, they was there," sighed Hawkins, "but every bloomin' million was represented by a certified check, an' payable in London !"

" By Jingo !" cried Morgan.   " What fearful luck !   But you had the prima donna's jewels."

" Yes," said Hawkins, with a moan. " But they was like all other prima donna's jewels—for advertisin' purposes only, an' made o' gum-arabic !"

"Horrible !" said Abeuchapeta. "And the crew, what did they say ?"

"They was a crew of a few words," sighed Hawkins. "Werry few words, an' not a civil word in the lot—mostly adjectives of a profane kind. When I told 'em what had happened, they got mad at Fortune for a-jiltin' of 'em, an'—well, I came here. I was 'sas'inated that werry night!"

"They killed you ?" cried Morgan.

"A dozen times," nodded Hawkins. "They always was a lavish lot. I met death in all its most horrid forms. First they stabbed me, then they shot me, then they clubbed me, and so on, endin' up with a lynchin'—but I didn't mind much after the first, which hurt a bit. But now that I'm here I'm glad it happened. This life is sort of less responsible than that other. You can't hurt a ghost by shooting him, because there ain't nothing to hurt, an' I must say I like bein' a mere vision what everybody can see through."

"All of which interesting tale proves what ?" queried Abeuchapeta.

"That piracy on the sea is not profitable in these days of the check banking system," said Kidd. "If you can get a chance at real gold it's all right, but it's of no earthly use to steal checks that people can stop payment on. Therefore it was my plan to visit the cities and do a little freebooting there, where solid material wealth is to be found."

"Well? Can't we do it now?" asked Abeuchapeta.

"Not with these women tagging after us," returned Kidd. "If we went to London and lifted the whole Bank of England, these women would have it spent on Regent Street inside of twenty-four hours."

"Then leave them on board," said Abeuchapeta.

"And have them steal the ship!" retorted Kidd. "No. There are but two things to do. Take 'em back, or land them in Paris. Tell them to spend a week on shore while we are provisioning. Tell 'em to shop to their hearts' content, and while they are doing it we can sneak off and leave them stranded."

" Splendid!" cried Morgan.

" But will they consent ?" asked Abeu-chapeta.

" Consent! To shop? In Paris? For a week ?" cried Morgan.

" Ha, ha!" laughed Hawkins. "Will they consent! Will a duck swim ?"

And so it was decided, which was the first incident in the career of the House-boat upon which the astute Mr. Sherlock Holmes had failed to count.

VI

A CONFERENCE BELOW-STAIRS

WHEN, with a resounding slam, the door to the upper deck of the House-boat was shut in the faces of queens Elizabeth and Cleopatra by the unmannerly Kidd, these ladies turned and gazed at those who thronged the stairs behind them in blank amazement, and the heart of Xanthippe, had one chosen to gaze through that diaphanous person's ribs, could have been seen to beat angrily.

Queen Elizabeth was so excited at this wholly novel attitude towards her regal self that, having turned, she sat down plump upon the floor in the most unroyal fashion.

"Well!" she ejaculated. "If this does not surpass everything! The idea of it!

Oh for one hour of my olden power, one hour of the axe, one hour of the block !"

" Get up," retorted Cleopatra, "and let us all return to the billiard-room and discuss this matter calmly. It is quite evident that something has happened of which we wotted little when we came aboard this craft."

" That is a good idea," said Calpurnia, retreating below. " I can see through the window that we are in motion. The vessel has left her moorings, and is making considerable headway down the stream, and the distinctly masculine voices we have heard are indications to my mind that the ship is manned, and that this is the result of design rather than of accident. Let us below."

Elizabeth rose up and readjusted her ruff, which in the excitement of the moment had been forced to assume a position about her forehead which gave one the impression that its royal wearer had suddenly donned a sombrero.

QUEEN ELIZABETH DESIRES AN AXE AND ONE HOUR OF HER OLDEN POWER

"Very well," she said. "Let us below ; but oh, for the axe !"

"Bring the lady an axe," cried Xanthippe, sarcastically. "She wants to cut somebody."

The sally was not greeted with applause. The situation was regarded as being too serious to admit of humor, and in silence they filed back into the billiard-room, and, arranging themselves in groups, stood about anxiously discussing the situation.

"It's getting rougher every minute," sobbed Ophelia. "Look at those pool-balls !" These were in very truth chasing each other about the table in an extraordinary fashion. "And I wish I'd never followed you horrid new creatures on board !" the poor girl added, in an agony of despair.

"I believe we've crossed the bar already !" said Cleopatra, gazing out of the window at a nasty choppy sea that was adding somewhat to the disquietude of the fair gathering. "If this is merely a joke on the part of the Associated Shades, it is a mighty poor one, and I think it is time it should cease."

" Oh, for an axe !" moaned Elizabeth, again.

"Excuse me, your Majesty," put in Xanthippe. " You said that before, and I must say it is getting tiresome. You couldn't do anything with an axe. Suppose you had one. What earthly good would it do you, who were accustomed to doing all your killing by proxy ? I don't believe, if you had the unmannerly person who slammed the door in your face lying prostrate upon the billiard-table here, you could hit him a square blow in the neck if you had a hundred axes. Delilah might as well cry for her scissors, for all the good it would do us in our predicament. If Cleopatra had her asp with her it might be more to the purpose. One deadly little snake like that let loose on the upper deck would doubtless drive these boors into the sea, and even then our condition would not be bettered, for

there isn't any of us that can sail a boat.
There isn't an old salt among us.

"Too bad Mrs. Lot isn't along," gig-
gled Marguerite de Valois, whose Gallic
spirits were by no means overshadowed by
the unhappy predicament in which she
found herself.

"I'm here," piped up Mrs. Lot.   "But
I'm not that kind of a salt."

"I am present," said Mrs. Noah.
"Though why I ever came I don't know,
for I vowed the minute I set my foot on
Ararat that dry land was good enough for
me, and that I'd never step aboard another boat as long as I lived.   If, however, now that I am here, I can give you
the benefit of my nautical experience,
you are all perfectly welcome to it."

"I'm sure we're very much obliged
for the offer," said Portia, "but in the
emergency which has arisen we cannot
say how much obliged we are until we
know what your experience amounted to.
Before relying upon you we ought to
know how far that reliance can go—not

that I lack confidence in you, my dear madam, but that in an hour of peril one must take care to rely upon the oak, not upon the reed."

"The point is properly taken," said Elizabeth, "and I wish to say here that I am easier in my mind when I realize that we have with us so level-headed a person as the lady who has just spoken. She has spoken truly and to the point. If I were to become queen again, I should make her my attorney-general. We must not go ahead impulsively, but look at all things in a calm, judicial manner."

"Which is pretty hard work with a sea like this on," remarked Ophelia, faintly, for she was getting a trifle sallow, as indeed she might, for the House-boat was beginning to roll tremendously, with no alleviation save an occasional pitch, which was an alleviation only in the sense that it gave variety to their discomfort. "I don't believe a chief-justice could look at things calmly and in a judicial manner if he felt as I do."

"Poor dear!" said the matronly Mrs. Noah, sympathetically. "I know exactly how you feel. I have been there myself. The fourth day out I and my whole family were in the same condition, except that Noah, my husband, was so very far gone that I could not afford to yield. I nursed him for six days before he got his sea-legs on, and then succumbed myself."

"But," gasped Ophelia, "that doesn't help me—"

"It did my husband," said Mrs. Noah. "When he heard that the boys were sea-sick too, he actually laughed and began to get better right away. There is really only one cure for the *mal de mer,* and that is the fun of knowing that somebody else is suffering too. If some of you ladies would kindly yield to the seductions of the sea, I think we could get this poor girl on her feet in an instant."

Unfortunately for poor Ophelia, there was no immediate response to this appeal, and the unhappy young woman was forced to suffer in solitude.

"We have no time for untimely diversions of this sort," snapped Xanthippe, with a scornful glance at the suffering Ophelia, who, having retired to a comfortable lounge at an end of the room, was evidently improving.   "I have no sympathy with this habit some of my sex seem to have acquired of succumbing to an immediate sensation of this nature."

"I hope to be pardoned for interrupting," said Mrs. Noah, with a great deal of firmness, "but I wish Mrs. Socrates to understand that it is rather early in the voyage for her to lay down any such broad principle as that, and for her own sake to-morrow, I think it would be well if she withdrew the sentiment.   There are certain things about a sea-voyage that are more or less beyond the control of man or woman, and any one who chides that poor suffering child on yonder sofa ought to be more confident than Mrs. Socrates can possibly be that within an hour she will not be as badly off.   People who live in glass houses should not throw dice."

"I shall never yield to anything so undignified as seasickness, let me tell you that," retorted Xanthippe. "Furthermore, the proverb is not as the lady has quoted it. 'People who live in glass houses should not throw stones' is the proper version."

"I was not quoting," returned Mrs. Noah, calmly. "When I said that people who live in glass houses should not throw dice, I meant precisely what I said. People who live in glass houses should not take chances. In assuming with such vainglorious positiveness that she will not be seasick, the lady who has just spoken is giving tremendous odds, as the boys used to say on the Ark when we gathered about the table at night and began to make small wagers on the day's run."

"I think we had better suspend this discussion," suggested Cleopatra. "It is of no immediate interest to any one but Ophelia, and I fancy she does not care to dwell upon it at any great length. It is more important that we should de—

7

cide upon our future course of action.
In the first place, the question is who
these people up on deck are. If they are
the members of the club, we are all right.
They will give us our scare, and land us
safely again at the pier.   In that event it
is our womanly duty to manifest no con-
cern, and to seem to be aware of nothing
unusual in the proceeding.   It would
never do to let them think that their joke
has been a good one. If, on the other
hand, as I fear, we are the victims of some
horde of ruffians, who have pounced upon
us unawares, and are going into the business of abduction on a wholesale basis, we
must meet treachery with treachery, strategy with strategy.   I, for one, am perfectly willing to make every man on board
walk the plank, having confidence in the
seawomanship of Mrs. Noah and her abil-
ity to steer us into port."

"I am quite in accord with these
views," put in Madame Récamier, "and
I move you, Mrs. President, that we or-
ganize a series of subcommittees—one on

treachery, with Lucretia Borgia and Delilah as members; one on strategy, consist-
ing of Portia and Queen Elizabeth; one
on navigation, headed by Mrs. Noah; with
a final subcommittee on reconnoitre, with
Cassandra to look forward, and Mrs. Lot
to look aft—all of these subordinated to
a central committee of safety headed by
Cleopatra and Caïpurnia.   The rest of us
can then commit ourselves and our interests unreservedly to these ladies, and proceed to enjoy ourselves without thought
of the morrow."

"I second the motion," said Ophelia,
"with the amendment that Madame Récamier be appointed chair-lady of another
subcommittee, on entertainment."

The amendment was accepted, and the
motion put.   It was carried with an en-
thusiastic aye, and the organization was
complete.

The various committees retired to the
several corners of the room to discuss
their individual lines of action, when a
shadow was observed to obscure the

moonlight which had been streaming in through the window. The faces of Calpurnia and Cleopatra blanched for an instant, as, immediately following upon this apparition, a large bundle was hurled through the open port into the middle of the room, and the shadow vanished.

"Is it a bomb ?" cried several of the ladies at once.

"Nonsense !" said Madame Récamier, jumping lightly forward. " A man doesn't mind blowing a woman up, but he'll never blow himself up. We're safe enough in that respect. The thing looks to me like a bundle of illustrated papers."

" That's what it is," said Cleopatra, who had been investigating. " It's rather a discourteous bit of courtesy, tossing them in through the window that way, I think, but I presume they mean well. Dear me," she added, as, having untied the bundle, she held one of the open papers up before her, "how interesting ! All the latest Paris fashions. Humph ! Look at those sleeves, Elizabeth. What an impregnable fortress you would have been with those sleeves added to your ruffs!"

"I should think they'd be very becoming," put in Cassandra, standing on her tiptoes and looking over Cleopatra's shoulder. "That Watteau isn't bad, either, is it, now?"

"No," remarked Calpurnia. "I wonder how a Watteau back like that would go on my blue alpaca?"

"Very nicely," said Elizabeth. "How many gores has it?"

"Five," observed Calpurnia. "One more than Cæsar's toga. We had to have our costumes distinct in some way."

"A remarkable hat, that," nodded Mrs. Lot, her eye catching sight of a Virot creation at the top of the page.

"Reminds me of Eve's description of an autumn scene in the garden," smiled Mrs. Noah. "Gorgeous in its foliage, beautiful thing; though I shouldn't have dared wear one in the Ark, with all those hungry animals browsing about the upper and lower decks."

"I wonder," remarked Cleopatra, as she cocked her head to one side to take in the full effect of an attractive summer gown—"I wonder how that waist would make up in blue crépon, with a yoke of lace and a stylishly contrasting stock of satin ribbon?"

"It would depend upon how you finished the sleeves," remarked Madame Récamier. "If you had a few puffs of rich brocaded satin set in with deeply folded pleats it wouldn't be bad."

"I think it would be very effective," observed Mrs. Noah, "but a trifle too light for general wear. I should want some kind of a wrap with it."

"It does need that," assented Elizabeth. "A wrap made of passementerie and jet, with a mousseline de soie ruche about the neck held by a *chou*, would make it fascinating."

"The committee on treachery is ready to report," said Delilah, rising from her corner, where she and Lucretia Borgia had been having so animated a discussion

"'THE COMMITTEE ON TREACHERY IS READY TO REPORT'"

that they had failed to observe the others crowding about Cleopatra and the papers.

"A little sombre," said Cleopatra. "The corsage is effective, but I don't like those basque terminations. I've never approved of those full godets—"

"The committee on treachery," remarked Delilah again, raising her voice, "has a suggestion to make."

"I can't get over those sleeves, though," laughed Helen of Troy. "What is the use of them?"

"They might be used to get Greeks into Troy," suggested Madame Récamier.

"The committee on treachery," roared Delilah, thoroughly angered by the absorption of the chairman and others, "has a suggestion to make. This is the third and last call."

"Oh, I beg pardon," cried Cleopatra, rapping for order. "I had forgotten all about our committees. Excuse me, Delilah. I—ah—was absorbed in other matters. Will you kindly lay your pattern— I should say your plan—before us?"

" It is briefly this," said Delilah.   " It has been suggested that we invite the crew of this vessel to a chafing-dish party, under the supervision of Lucretia Borgia, and that she—"

The balance of the plan was not outlined, for at this point the speaker was interrupted by a loud knocking at the door, its instant opening, and the appearance in the doorway of that ill-visaged ruffian Captain Kidd.

"Ladies," he began, " I have come here to explain to you the situation in which you find yourselves. Have I your permission to speak ?"

The ladies started back, but the chairman was equal to the occasion.

" Go on," said Cleopatra, with queenly dignity, turning to the interloper ; and the pirate proceeded to take the second step in the nefarious plan upon which he and his brother ruffians had agreed, of which the tossing in through the window of the bundle of fashion papers was the first.

VII

IT was about twenty-four hours after
the events narrated in the preceding
chapters that Mr. Sherlock Holmes as-
sumed command of the *Gehenna*, which
was nothing more nor less than the shadow of the ill-starred ocean steamship *City
of Chicago*, which tried some years ago to
reach Liverpool by taking the overland
route through Ireland, fortunately without detriment to her passengers or crew,
who had the pleasure of the experience of
shipwreck without any of the discomforts
of drowning. As will be remembered, the
obstructionist nature of the Irish soil prevented the *City of Chicago* from proceeding farther inland than was necessary to
keep her well balanced amidships upon a

convenient and not too stony bed ; and
that after a brief sojourn on the rocks
she was finally disposed of to the Styx
Navigation Company, under which title
Charon had had himself incorporated, is
a matter of nautical history. The change
of name to the *Gehenna* was the act of
Charon himself, and was prompted, no
doubt, by a desire to soften the jealous
prejudices of the residents of the Stygian
capital against the flourishing and ever-
growing metropolis of Illinois.

The Associated Shades had had some
trouble in getting this craft. Charon,
through his constant association with life
on both sides of the dark river, had gained
a knowledge, more or less intimate, of
modern business methods, and while as
janitor of the club he was subject to the
will of the House Committee, and sym-
pathized deeply with the members of the
association in their trouble, as president of the Styx Navigation Company he
was bound up in certain newly attained
commercial ideas which were embarrass-

ing to those members of the association
to whose hands the chartering of a vessel
had been committed.

"See here, Charon," Sir Walter Raleigh
had said, after Charon had expressed himself as deeply sympathetic, but unable to
shave the terms upon which the vessel
could be had, "you are an infernal old
hypocrite. You go about wringing your
hands over our misfortunes until they've
got as dry and flabby as a pair of kid
gloves, and yet when we ask you for a
ship of suitable size and speed to go out
after those pirates, you become a sort of
twin brother to Shylock, without his excuse. His instincts are accidents of
birth. Yours are cultivated, and you
know it."

"You are very much mistaken, Sir
Walter," Charon had answered to this.
"You don't understand my position. It
is a very hard one. As janitor of your
club I am really prostrated over the
events of the past twenty-four hours.
My occupation is gone, and my despair

over your loss is correspondingly greater, for I have time on my hands to brood over it. I was hysterical as a woman yesterday afternoon—so hysterical that I came near upsetting one of the Furies who engaged me to row her down to Madame Medusa's villa last evening; and right at the sluice of the vitriol reservoir at that."

"Then why the deuce don't you do something to help us?" pleaded Hamlet.

"How can I do any more than I have done? I've offered you the *Gehenna*," retorted Charon.

"But on what terms?" expostulated Raleigh. "If we had all the wealth of the Indies we'd have difficulty in paying you the sums you demand."

"But I am only president of the company," explained Charon. "I'd like, as president, to show you some courtesy, and I'm perfectly willing to do so; but when it comes down to giving you a vessel like that, I'm bound by my official oath to consider the interest of the stockholders.

" ' YOU ARE VERY MUCH MISTAKEN, SIR WALTER ' "

It isn't as it used to be when I had boats to hire in my own behalf alone.   In those days I had nobody's interest but my own to look after.   Now the ships all belong to the Styx Navigation Company.   Can't you see the difference ?"

" You own all the stock, don't you ?" insisted Raleigh.

" I don't know," Charon answered, blandly.   " I haven't seen the transfer-books lately."

" But you know that you did own every share of it, and that you haven't sold any, don't you ?" put in Hamlet.

Charon was puzzled for a moment, but shortly his face cleared, and Sir Walter's heart sank, for it was evident that the old fellow could not be cornered.

" Well, it's this way, Sir Walter, and your Highness,—" he said, " I—I can't say whether any of that stock has been trans-ferred or not.   The fact is, I've been spec-ulating a little on margin, and I've put up that stock as security, and, for all I know, I may have been sold out by my brokers.

I've been so upset by this unfortunate oc-
currence that I haven't seen the market
reports for two days.   Really you'll have
to be content with my offer or go without the *Gehenna*.   There's too much suspicion attached to high corporate officials
lately for me to yield a jot in the position
I have taken.   It would never do to get
you all ready to start, and then have an
injunction clapped on you by some un-
foreseen stockholder who was not satisfied
with the terms offered you ; nor can I
ever let it be said of me that to retain my
position as janitor of your organization I
sacrificed a trust committed to my charge.
I'll gladly lend you my private launch,
though I don't think it will aid you much,
because the naphtha-tank has exploded,
and the screw slipped off and went to the
bottom two weeks ago.   Still, it is at your
service, and I've no doubt that either
Phidias or Benvenuto Cellini will carve
out a paddle for you if you ask him to."

"Bah!" retorted Raleigh.   "You might
as well offer us a pair of skates."

"I would, if I thought the river 'd freeze," retorted Charon, blandly.

Raleigh and Hamlet turned away impatiently and left Charon to his own devices, which for the time being consisted largely of winking his other eye quietly and outwardly making a great show of grief.

"He's too canny for us, I am afraid," said Sir Walter. "We'll have to pay him his money."

"Let us first consult Sherlock Holmes," suggested Hamlet, and this they proceeded at once to do.

"There is but one thing to be done," observed the astute detective after he had heard Sir Walter's statement of the case. "It is an old saying that one should fight fire with fire. We must meet modern business methods with modern commercial ideas. Charter his vessel at his own price."

"But we'd never be able to pay," said Hamlet.

"Ha - ha!" laughed Holmes. "It is

evident that you know nothing of the laws of trade nowadays. Don't pay!"

"But how can we?" asked Raleigh.

"The method is simple. You haven't anything to pay with," returned Holmes. "Let him sue. Suppose he gets a verdict. You haven't anything he can attach—if you have, make it over to your wives or your fiancées."

"Is that honest?" asked Hamlet, shaking his head doubtfully.

"It's business," said Holmes.

"But suppose he wants an advance payment?" queried Hamlet.

"Give him a check drawn to his own order. He'll have to endorse it when he deposits it, and that will make him responsible," laughed Holmes.

"What a simple thing when you understand it!" commented Raleigh.

"Very," said Holmes. "Business is getting by slow degrees to be an exact science. It reminds me of the Brighton mystery, in which I played a modest part some ten years ago, when I first took up

ferreting as a profession. I was sitting
one night in my room at one of the Brighton hotels, which shall be nameless. I
never give the name of any of the hotels
at which I stop, because it might give of-
fence to the proprietors of other hotels,
with the result that my books would be
excluded from sale therein. Suffice it to
say that I was spending an early summer
Sunday at Brighton with my friend Watson. We had dined well, and were enjoying our evening smoke together upon a
small balcony overlooking the water, when
there came a timid knock on the door of
my room.

" ' Watson,' said I, 'here comes some
one for advice. Do you wish to wager a
small bottle upon it ?'

" ' Yes,' he answered, with a smile. ' I
am thirsty and I'd like a small bottle; and
while I do not expect to win, I'll take the
bet. I should like to know, though, how
you know.'

" ' It is quite simple,' said I. ' The
timidity of the knock shows that my vis-
8

itor is one of two classes of persons—an
autograph-hunter or a client, one of the
two.   You see I give you a chance to win.
It may be an autograph - hunter, but I
think it is a client.   If it were a creditor,
he would knock boldly, even ostentatious-
ly; if it were the maid, she would not
knock at all; if it were the hall-boy, he
would not come until I had rung five
times for him.   None of these things has
occurred; the knock is the half-hearted
knock which betokens either that the
person who knocked is in trouble, or is
uncertain as to his reception.   I am willing, however, considering the heat and
my desire to quench my thirst, to wager
that it is a client.'

"'Done,' said Watson; and I immediately remarked, 'Come in.'

"The door opened, and a man of about
thirty-five years of age, in a bathing-suit,
entered the room, and I saw at a glance
what had happened.

"'Your name is Burgess,' I said.
'You came here from London this morn-

ing, expecting to return to-night. You
brought no luggage with you. After
luncheon you went in bathing. You had
machine No. 35, and when you came out
of the water you found that No. 35 had
disappeared, with your clothes and the
silver watch your uncle gave you on the
day you succeeded to his business.'

"Of course, gentlemen," observed the
detective, with a smile at Sir Walter and
Hamlet — "of course the man fairly
gasped, and I continued : 'You have
been lying face downward in the sand
ever since, waiting for nightfall, so that
you could come to me for assistance, not
considering it good form to make an afternoon call upon a stranger at his hotel,
clad in a bathing-suit. Am I correct?'

"'Sir,' he replied, with a look of wonder, 'you have narrated my story exactly
as it happened, and I find I have made
no mistake in coming to you. Would you
mind telling me what is your course of
reasoning ?'

"'It is plain as day,' said I. 'I am

the person with the red beard with whom you came down third class from London this morning, and you told me your name was Burgess and that you were a butcher.   When you looked to see the time, I remarked upon the oddness of your watch, which led to your telling me that it was the gift of your uncle.'

" ' True,' said Burgess, ' but I did not tell you I had no luggage.'

" ' No,' said I, ' but that you hadn't is plain ; for if you had brought any other clothing besides that you had on with you, you would have put it on to come here.   That you have been robbed I deduce also from your costume.'

" ' But the number of the machine ?' asked Watson.

" ' Is on the tag on the key hanging about his neck,' said I.

" ' One more question,' queried Burgess.   ' How do you know I have been lying face downward on the beach ever since ?'

" ' By the sand in your eyebrows,' I replied ; and Watson ordered up the small bottle."

"I fail to see what it was in our conversation, however," observed Hamlet, somewhat impatient over the delay caused by the narration of this tale, "that suggested this train of thought to you."

"The sequel will show," returned Holmes.

"Oh, Lord!" put in Raleigh. "Can't we put off the sequel until a later issue ? Remember, Mr. Holmes, that we are constantly losing time."

"The sequel is brief, and I can narrate it on our way to the office of the Navigation Company," observed the detective. "When the bottle came I invited Mr. Burgess to join us, which he did, and as the hour was late when we came to separate, I offered him the use of my parlor overnight. This he accepted, and we retired.

"The next morning when I arose to dress, the mystery was cleared."

"You had dreamed its solution?" asked Raleigh.

"No," replied Holmes. "Burgess had disappeared with all my clothing, my false-beard, my suit-case, and my watch. The only thing he had left me was the bathing-suit and a few empty small bottles."

"And why, may I ask," put in Hamlet, as they drew near to Charon's office— "why does that case remind you of business as it is conducted to-day?"

"In this, that it is a good thing to stay out of unless you know it all," explained Holmes. "I omitted in the case of Burgess to observe one thing about him. Had I observed that his nose was rectilinear, incurved, and with a lifted base, and that his auricular temporal angle was between 96 and 97 degrees, I should have known at once that he was an impostor. *Vide* Ottolenghui on 'Ears and Noses I Have Met,' pp. 631–640."

"Do you mean to say that you can tell a criminal by his ears?" demanded Hamlet.

"IN THE DEAD OF NIGHT SHYLOCK HAD STOLEN UP THE
GANG-PLANK"

"If he has any—yes; but I did not know that at the time of the Brighton mystery. Therefore I should have stayed out of the case. But here we are. Good-morning, Charon."

By this time the trio had entered the private office of the president of the Styx Navigation Company, and in a few moments the vessel was chartered at a fabulous price.

On the return to the wharf, Sir Walter somewhat nervously asked Holmes if he thought the plan they had settled upon would work.

"Charon is a very shrewd old fellow," said he. "He may outwit us yet."

"The chances are just two and one-eighth degrees in your favor," observed Holmes, quietly, with a glance at Raleigh's ears. "The temporal angle of your ears is $93\frac{1}{8}$ degrees, whereas Charon's stand out at 91, by my otometer. To that extent your criminal instincts are superior to his. If criminology is an exact science, reasoning by your respective ears,

you ought to beat him out by a perceptible though possibly narrow margin."

With which assurance Raleigh went
ahead with his preparations, and within
twelve hours the *Gehenna* was under way,
carrying a full complement of crew and
officers, with every state-room on board
occupied by some spirit of the more illustrious kind.

Even Shylock was on board, though no
one knew it, for in the dead of night he
had stolen quietly up the gang-plank and
had hidden himself in an empty water-
cask in the forecastle.

"'Tisn't Venice," he said, as he sat
down and breathed heavily through the
bung of the barrel, "but it's musty and
damp enough, and, considering the cost,
I can't complain. You can't get something for nothing, even in Hades."

VIII

ON BOARD THE "GEHENNA"

WHEN the *Gehenna* had passed down
the Styx and out through the beautiful
Cimmerian Harbor into the broad waters
of the ocean, and everything was comparatively safe for a while at least, Sherlock Holmes came down from the bridge,
where he had taken his place as the commander of the expedition at the moment
of departure. His brow was furrowed
with anxiety, and through his massive
forehead his brain could be seen to be
throbbing violently, and the corrugations
of his gray matter were not pleasant to
witness as he tried vainly to squeeze an
idea out of them.

"What is the matter?" asked Demosthenes, anxiously. "We are not in any
danger, are we?"

"No," replied Holmes. "But I am somewhat puzzled at the bubbles on the surface of the ocean, and the ripples which we passed over an hour or two ago, barely perceptible through the most powerful microscope, indicate to my mind that for some reason at present unknown to me the House-boat has changed her course. Take that bubble floating by. It is the last expiring bit of aerial agitation of the House-boat's wake. Observe whence it comes. Not from the Azores quarter, but as if instead of steering a straight course thither the House-boat had taken a sharp turn to the northeast, and was making for Havre ; or, in other words, Paris instead of London seems to have become their destination."

Demosthenes looked at Holmes with blank amazement, and, to keep from stammering out the exclamation of wonder that rose to his lips, he opened his *bonbonnière* and swallowed a pebble.

"You don't happen to have a cocaine

tablet in your box, do you?" queried
Holmes.

"No," returned the Greek. "Cocaine
makes me flighty and nervous, but these
pebbles sort of ballast me and hold me
down. How on earth do you know that
that bubble comes from the wake of the
House-boat?"

"By my chemical knowledge, merely,"
replied Holmes. "A merely worldly vessel
leaves a phosphorescent bubble in its wake.
That one we have just discovered is not
so, but sulphurescent, if I may coin a word
which it seems to me the English lan-
guage is very much in need of. It proves,
then, that the bubble is a portion of the
wake of a Stygian craft, and the only
Stygian craft that has cleared the Cimmerian Harbor for years is the House-
boat—Q. E. D."

"We can go back until we find the ripple again, and follow that, I presume,"
sneered Le Coq, who did not take much
stock in the theories of his great rival,
largely because he was a detective by in-

tuition rather than by study of the science.

"You can if you want to, but it is better not to," rejoined Holmes, simply, as though not observing the sneer, "because the ripple represents the outer lines of the angle of disturbance in the water; and as any one of the sides to an angle is greater than the perpendicular from the hypothenuse to the apex, you'd merely be going the long way. This is especially important when you consider the formation of the bow of the House-boat, which is rounded like the stern of most vessels, and comes near to making a pair of ripples at an angle of ninety degrees."

"Then," observed Sir Walter, with a sigh of disappointment, "we must change our course and sail for Paris?"

"I am afraid so," said Holmes; "but of course it's by no means certain as yet. I think if Columbus would go up into the mizzentop and look about him, he might discover something either in confirmation or refutation of the theory."

"He couldn't discover anything," put in Pinzon. "He never did."

"Well, I like that!" retorted Columbus. "I'd like to know who discovered America."

"So should I," observed Leif Ericson, with a wink at Vespucci.

"Tut!" retorted Columbus. "I did it, and the world knows it, whether you claim it or not."

"Yes, just as Noah discovered Ararat," replied Pinzon. "You sat upon the deck until we ran plumb into an island, after floating about for three months, and then you couldn't tell it from a continent, even when you had it right before your eyes. Noah might just as well have told his family that he discovered a roof garden as for you to go back to Spain telling 'em all that San Salvador was the United States."

"Well, I don't care," said Columbus, with a short laugh. "I'm the one they celebrate, so what's the odds? I'd rather stay down here in the smoking-room enjoying a small game, anyhow, than climb up that mast and strain my eyes for ten or a dozen hours looking for evidence to prove or disprove the correctness of another man's theory. I wouldn't know evidence when I saw it, anyhow. Send Judge Blackstone."

"I draw the line at the mizzentop," observed Blackstone. "The dignity of the bench must and shall be preserved, and I'll never consent to climb up that rigging, getting pitch and paint on my ermine, no matter who asks me to go."

"Whomsoever I tell to go, shall go," put in Holmes, firmly. "I am commander of this ship. It will pay you to remember that, Judge Blackstone."

"And I am the Court of Appeals," retorted Blackstone, hotly. "Bear that in mind, captain, when you try to send me up. I'll issue a writ of *habeas corpus* on my own body, and commit you for contempt."

"There's no use of sending the Judge, anyhow," said Raleigh, fearing by the

JUDGE BLACKSTONE REFUSES TO CLIMB TO THE MIZZENTOP

glitter that came into the eye of the commander that trouble might ensue unless pacificatory measures were resorted to. "He's accustomed to weighing everything carefully, and cannot be rushed into a decision. If he saw any evidence, he'd have to sit on it a week before reaching a conclusion. What we need here more than anything else is an expert seaman, a lookout, and I nominate Shem. He has sailed under his father, and I have it on good authority that he is a nautical expert."

Holmes hesitated for an instant. He was considering the necessity of disciplining the recalcitrant Blackstone, but he finally yielded.

"Very well," he said. "Shem be it. Bo'sun, pipe Shem on deck, and tell him that general order number one requires him to report at the mizzentop right away, and that immediately he sees anything he shall come below and make it known to me. As for the rest of us, having a very considerable appetite, I do now decree that it is dinner-time. Shall we go below?"

"I don't think I care for any, thank you," said Raleigh. "Fact is — ah — I dined last week, and am not hungry."

Noah laughed. "Oh, come below and watch us eat, then," he said. "It 'll do you good."

But there was no reply. Raleigh had plunged head first into his state-room, which fortunately happened to be on the upper deck. The rest of the spirits repaired below to the saloon, where they were soon engaged in an animated discussion of such viands as the larder provided.

"This," said Dr. Johnson, from the head of the table, "is what I call comfort. I don't know that I am so anxious to recover the House-boat, after all."

"Nor I," said Socrates, "with a ship like this to go off cruising on, and with such a larder. Look at the thickness of that purée, Doctor—"

"Excuse me," said Boswell, faintly, "but I—I've left my note-bub-book up-

SHEM IN THE LOOKOUT

stairs, Doctor, and I'd like to go up and get it."

"Certainly," said Dr. Johnson. "I judge from your color, which is highly suggestive of a modern magazine poster, that it might be well too if you stayed on deck for a little while and made a few entries in your commonplace book."

"Thank you," said Boswell, gratefully. "Shall you say anything clever during dinner, sir? If so, I might be putting it down while I'm up—"

"Get out!" roared the Doctor. "Get up as high as you can—get up with Shem on the mizzentop—"

"Very good, sir," replied Boswell, and he was off.

"You ought to be more lenient with him, Doctor," said Bonaparte; "he means well."

"I know it," observed Johnson; "but he's so very previous. Last winter, at Chaucer's dinner to Burns, I made a speech, which Boswell printed a week before it was delivered, with the words

9

'laughter' and 'uproarious applause' interspersed through it. It placed me in a false position."

"How did he know what you were going to say?" queried Demosthenes.

"Don't know," replied Johnson. "Kind of mind-reader, I fancy," he added, blushing a trifle. "But, Captain Holmes, what do you deduce from your observation of the wake of the House-boat? If she's going to Paris, why the change?"

"I have two theories," replied the detective.

"Which is always safe," said Le Coq.

"Always; it doubles your chances of success," acquiesced Holmes. "Anyhow, it gives you a choice, which makes it more interesting. The change of her course from Londonward to Parisward proves to me either that Kidd is not satisfied with the extent of the revenge he has already taken, and wishes to ruin you gentlemen financially by turning your wives, daughters, and sisters loose on the Parisian shops, or that the pirates have themselves been overthrown by the ladies, who have decided to prolong their cruise and get some fun out of their misfortune."

"And where else than to Paris would any one in search of pleasure go?" asked Bonaparte.

"I had more fun a few miles outside of Brussels," said Wellington, with a sly wink at Washington.

"Oh, let up on that!" retorted Bonaparte. "It wasn't you beat me at Waterloo. You couldn't have beaten me at a plain ordinary game of old-maid with a stacked pack of cards, much less in the game of war, if you hadn't had the elements with you."

"Tut!" snapped Wellington. "It was clear science laid you out, Boney."

"Taisey-voo!" shouted the irate Corsican. "Clear science be hanged! Wet science was what did it. If it hadn't been for the rain, my little Duke, I should have been in London within a week, my grenadiers would have been camping in your Rue Peekadeely, and the Old Guard all over everywhere else."

" You must have had a gay army, then," laughed Cæsar. " What are French soldiers made of, that they can't stand the wet—unshrunk linen or flannel ?"

" Bah !" observed Napoleon, shrugging his shoulders and walking a few paces away. " You do not understand the French. The Frenchman is not a pell-mell soldier like you Romans; he is the poet of arms ; he does not go in for glory at the expense of his dignity ; style, form, is dearer to him than honor, and he has no use for fighting in the wet and coming out of the fight conspicuous as a victor with the curl out of his feathers and his epaulets rusted with the damp. There is no glory in water. But if we had had umbrellas and mackintoshes, as every Englishman who comes to the Continent always has, and a bath-tub for everybody, then would your Waterloo have been different again, and the great democracy of Europe with a Bonaparte for emperor would have been founded for what the Americans call the keeps; and as for your little Great Britain, ha! she would have become the Blackwell's Island of the Greater France."

"You're almost as funny as *Punch* isn't," drawled Wellington, with an angry gesture at Bonaparte. "You weren't within telephoning distance of victory all day. We simply played with you, my boy. It was a regular game of golf for us. We let you keep up pretty close and win a few holes, but on the home drive we had you beaten in one stroke. Go to, my dear Bonaparte, and stop talking about the flood."

"It's a lucky thing for us that Noah wasn't a Frenchman, eh?" said Frederick the Great. "How that rain would have fazed him if he had been! The human race would have been wiped out."

"Oh, pshaw!" ejaculated Noah, deprecating the unseemliness of the quarrel, and putting his arm affectionately about Bonaparte's shoulder. "When you come down to that, I was French—as French as one could be in those days—and these

Gallic subjects of my friend here were,
every one of 'em, my lineal descendants,
and their hatred of rain was inherited di-
rectly from me, their ancestor."

"Are not we English as much your
descendants?" queried Wellington, arch-
ing his eyebrows.

"You are," said Noah, "but you take
after Mrs. Noah more than after me.
Water never fazes a woman, and your delight in tubs is an essentially feminine
trait.   The first thing Mrs. Noah carried
aboard was a laundry outfit, and then she
went back for rugs and coats and all sorts
of hand-baggage.   Gad, it makes me laugh
to this day when I think of it!   She looked
for all the world like an Englishman
travelling on the Continent as she walked
up the gang-plank behind the elephants,
each elephant with a Gladstone bag in his
trunk and a hat-box tied to his tail."   Here
the venerable old weather-prophet winked
at Munchausen, and the little quarrel
which had been imminent passed off in a
general laugh.

" Where's Boswell ? He ought to get
that anecdote," said Johnson.

" I've locked him up in the library,"
said Holmes. " He's in charge of the log,
and as I have a pretty good general idea
as to what is about to happen, I have
mapped out a skeleton of the plot and set
him to work writing it up." Here the
detective gave a sudden start, placed his
hand to his ear, listened intently for an
instant, and, taking out his watch and
glancing at it, added, quietly, " In three
minutes Shem will be in here to announce
a discovery, and one of great importance,
I judge, from the squeak."

The assemblage gazed earnestly at
Holmes for a moment.

" The squeak ?" queried Raleigh.

" Precisely," said Holmes. " The squeak
is what I said, and as I always say what I
mean, it follows logically that I meant
what I said."

" I heard no squeak," observed Dr.
Johnson ; " and, furthermore, I fail to see
how a squeak, if I had heard it, would

have portended a discovery of importance."

"It would not—to you," said Holmes; "but with me it is different. My hearing is unusually acute. I can hear the dropping of a pin through a stone wall ten feet thick; any sound within a mile of my eardrum vibrates thereon with an intensity which would surprise you, and it is by the use of cocaine that I have acquired this wonderfully acute sense. A property which dulls the senses of most people renders mine doubly apprehensive; therefore, gentlemen, while to you there was no auricular disturbance, to me there was. I heard Shem sliding down the mast a minute since. The fact that he slid down the mast instead of climbing down the rigging showed that he was in great haste, therefore he must have something to communicate of great importance."

"Why isn't he here already, then? It wouldn't take him two minutes to get from the deck here," asked the ever-suspicious Le Coq.

"It is simple," returned Holmes, calmly. "If you will go yourself and slide down that mast you will see. Shem has stopped for a little witch-hazel to soothe his burns. It is no cool matter sliding down a mast two hundred feet in height."

As Sherlock Holmes spoke the door burst open and Shem rushed in.

"A signal of distress, captain!" he cried.

"From what quarter—to larboard?" asked Holmes.

"No," returned Shem, breathless.

"Then it must be dead ahead," said Holmes.

"Why not to starboard?" asked Le Coq, dryly.

"Because," answered Holmes, confidently, "it never happens so. If you had ever read a truly exciting sea-tale, my dear Le Coq, you would have known that interesting things, and particularly signals of distress, are never seen except to larboard or dead ahead."

A murmur of applause greeted this retort, and Le Coq subsided.

"The nature of the signal ?" demanded Holmes.

"A black flag, skull and cross-bones down, at half-mast !" cried Shem, "and on a rock-bound coast !"

"They're marooned, by heavens !" shouted Holmes, springing to his feet and rushing to the deck, where he was joined immediately by Sir Walter, Dr. Johnson, Bonaparte, and the others.

"Isn't he a daisy ?" whispered Demosthenes to Diogenes as they climbed the stairs.

"He is more than that ; he's a blooming orchid," said Diogenes, with intense enthusiasm. "I think I'll get my X-ray lantern and see if he's honest."

IX

CAPTAIN KIDD MEETS WITH AN OBSTACLE

"EXCUSE me, your Majesty," remarked
Helen of Troy as Cleopatra accorded permission to Captain Kidd to speak, "I have
not been introduced to this gentleman nor
has he been presented to me, and I really
cannot consent to any proceeding so irreg-
ular as this. I do not speak to gentlemen
I have not met, nor do I permit them to
address me."

"Hear, hear!" cried Xanthippe. "I
quite agree with the principle of my young
friend from Troy. It may be that when
we claimed for ourselves all the rights of
men that the right to speak and be spoken
to by other men without an introduction
was included in the list, but I for one
have no desire to avail myself of the privi-

lege, especially when it's a horrid-look-
ing man like this."

Kidd bowed politely, and smiled so ter-
ribly that several of the ladies fainted.

"I will withdraw," he said, turning to
Cleopatra ; and it must be said that his
suggestion was prompted by his heartfelt
wish, for now that he found himself thus
conspicuously brought before so many
women, with falsehood on his lips, his
courage began to ooze.

"Not yet, please," answered the chair-
lady. "I imagine we can get about this
difficulty without much trouble."

"I think it a perfectly proper objection
too," observed Delilah, rising. "If we
ever needed etiquette we need it now.
But I have a plan which will obviate any
further difficulty. If there is no one
among us who is sufficiently well acquainted with the gentleman to present him
formally to us, I will for the time being
take upon myself the office of ship's bar-
ber and cut his hair. I understand that
it is quite the proper thing for barbers to

talk, while cutting their hair, to persons
to whom they have not been introduced.
And, besides, he really needs a hair-cut
badly. Thus I shall establish an acquaintance with the captain, after which I can
with propriety introduce him to the rest
of you."

"Perhaps the gentleman himself might
object to that," put in Queen Elizabeth.
"If I remember rightly, your last custom-
er was very much dissatisfied with the trim
you gave him."

"It will be unnecessary to do what
Delilah proposes," said Mrs. Noah, with
a kindly smile, as she rose up from the
corner in which she had been sitting, an
interested listener. "I can introduce the
gentleman to you all with perfect propriety. He's a member of my family.
His grandfather was the great-grandson
a thousand and eight times removed of
my son Shem's great-grandnephew on his
father's side. His relationship to me is
therefore obvious, though from what I
know of his reputation I think he takes

more after my husband's ancestors than my own. Willie, dear, these ladies are friends of mine. Ladies, this young man is one of my most famous descendants. He has been a man of many adventures, and he has been hanged once, which, far from making him undesirable as an acquaintance, has served merely to render him harmless, and therefore a safe person to know. Now, my son, go ahead and speak your piece."

The good old spirit sat down, and the scruples of the objectors having thus been satisfied, Captain Kidd began.

"Now that I know you all," he remarked, as pleasantly as he could under the circumstances, "I feel that I can speak more freely, and certainly with a great deal less embarrassment than if I were addressing a gathering of entire strangers. I am not much of a hand at speaking, and have always felt somewhat nonplussed at finding myself in a position of this nature. In my whole career I never experienced but one irresistible impulse to make a public address of any length, and that was upon that unhappy occasion to which the greatest and grandest of my great-grandmothers has alluded, and that only as the chain by which I was suspended in mid-air tightened about my vocal chords. At that moment I could have talked impromptu for a year, so fast and numerously did thoughts of the uttermost import surge upward into my brain ; but circumstances over which I had no control prevented the utterance of those thoughts, and that speech is therefore lost to the world."

"He has the gift of continuity," observed Madame Récamier.

"Ought to be in the United States Senate," smiled Elizabeth.

"I wish I could make up my mind as to whether he is outrageously handsome or desperately ugly," remarked Helen of Troy. "He fascinates me, but whether it is the fascination of liking or of horror I can't tell, and it's quite important."

"Ladies," resumed the captain, his un-

easiness increasing as he came to the
point, "I am but the agent of your respective husbands, *fiancés*, and other masculine guardians. The gentlemen who were
previously the tenants of this club-house
have delegated to me the important, and
I may add highly agreeable, task of showing you the world. They have noted of
late years the growth of that feeling of
unrest which is becoming every day more
and more conspicuous in feminine circles
in all parts of the universe—on the earth,
where women are clamoring to vote, and
to be allowed to go out late at night without an escort; in Hades, where, as you
are no doubt aware, the management of
the government has fallen almost wholly
into the hands of the Furies; and even in
the halls of Jupiter himself, where, I am
credibly informed, Juno has been taking
private lessons in the art of hurling
thunderbolts—information which the extraordinary quality of recent electrical
storms on the earth would seem to con-
firm. Thunderbolts of late years have

been cast hither and yon in a most erratic fashion, striking where they were least expected, as those of you who keep in touch with the outer world must be fully aware. Now, actuated by their usual broad and liberal motives, the men of Hades wish to meet the views of you ladies to just that extent that your views are based upon a wise selection, in turn based upon experience, and they have come to me and in so many words have said, ' Mr. Kidd, we wish the women of Hades to see the world. We want them to be satisfied. We do not like this constantly increasing spirit of unrest. We, who have seen all the life that we care to see, do not ourselves feel equal to the task of showing them about. We will pay you liberally if you will take our House-boat, which they have always been anxious to enter, and personally conduct our beloved ones to Paris, London, and elsewhere. Let them see as much of life as they can stand. Accord them every privilege. Spare no expense ; only bring

10

them back again to us safe and sound.'
These were their words, ladies. I asked
them why they didn't come along themselves, saying that even if they were tired
of it all, they should make some personal
sacrifice to your comfort; and they answered, reasonably and well, that they would
be only too glad to do so, but that they
feared they might unconsciously seem to
exert a repressing influence upon you.
'We want them to feel absolutely free,
Captain Kidd,' said they, 'and if we are
along they may not feel so.' The answer
was convincing, ladies, and I accepted the
commission."

"But we knew nothing of all this," interposed Elizabeth. "The subject was
not broached to us by our husbands,
brothers, *fiancés*, or fathers. My brother,
Sir Walter Raleigh—"

Cleopatra chuckled. "Brother! Brother's good," she said.

"Well, that's what he is," retorted
Elizabeth, quickly. "I promised to be a
sister to him, and I'm going to keep my

word. That's the kind of a queen I am. I was about to remark," Elizabeth added, turning to the captain, " that my brother, Sir Walter Raleigh, never even hinted at any such plan, and usually he asked my advice in matters of so great importance."

" That is easily accounted for, madame," retorted Kidd. " Sir Walter intended this as a little surprise for you, that is all. The arrangements were all placed in his hands, and it was he who bound us all to secrecy. None of the ladies were to be informed of it."

" It does not sound altogether plausible," interposed Portia. " If you ladies do not object, I should like to cross-examine this—ah—gentleman."

Kidd paled visibly. He was not prepared for any such trial ; however, he put as good a face on the matter as he could, and announced his willingness to answer any questions that he might be asked.

" Shall we put him under oath?" asked Cleopatra.

" As you please, ladies," said the pirate.

"A pirate's word is as good as his bond; but I'll take an oath if you choose—a half-dozen of 'em, if need be."

"I fancy we can get along without that," said Portia. "Now, Captain Kidd, who first proposed this plan?"

"Socrates," said Kidd, unblushingly, with a sly glance at Xanthippe.

"What ?" cried Xanthippe. "My husband propose anything that would contribute to my pleasure or intellectual advancement ? Bah! Your story is transparently false at the outset."

"Nevertheless," said Kidd, "the scheme was proposed by Socrates. He said a trip of that kind for Xanthippe would be very restful and health-giving."

"For me ?" cried Xanthippe, sceptically.

"No, madame, for him," retorted Kidd.

"Ah—ho-ho ! That's the way of it, eh ?" said Xanthippe, flushing to the roots of her hair. "Very likely. You —ah—you will excuse my doubting your

CAPTAIN KIDD CONSENTS TO BE CROSS-EXAMINED BY PORTIA

word, Captain Kidd, a moment since. I withdraw my remark, and in order to make fullest reparation, I beg to assure these ladies that I am now perfectly convinced that you are telling the truth. That last observation is just like my husband, and when I get back home again, if I ever do, well—ha, ha !—we'll have a merry time, that's all."

"And what was—ah—Bassanio's connection with this affair ?" added Portia, hesitatingly.

"He was not informed of it," said Kidd, archly. "I am not acquainted with Bassanio, my lady, but I overheard Sir Walter enjoining upon the others the absolute necessity of keeping the whole affair from Bassanio, because he was afraid he would not consent to it. 'Bassanio has a most beautiful wife, gentlemen,' said Sir Walter, 'and he wouldn't think of parting with her under any circumstances ; therefore let us keep our intentions a secret from him.' I did not hear whom the gentleman married, madame ;

but the others, Prince Hamlet, the Duke of Buckingham, and Louis the Fourteenth, all agreed that Mrs. Bassanio was too beautiful a person to be separated from, and that it was better, therefore, to keep Bassanio in the dark as to their little enterprise until it was too late for him to interfere."

A pink glow of pleasure suffused the lovely countenance of the cross-examiner, and it did not require a very sharp eye to see that the wily Kidd had completely won her over to his side. On the other hand, Elizabeth's brow became as corrugated as her ruff, and the spirit of the pirate shivered to the core as he turned and gazed upon that glowering face.

"Sir Walter agreed to that, did he?" snapped Elizabeth. "And yet he was willing to part with—ah—his sister."

"Well, your Majesty," began Kidd, hesitatingly, "you see it was this way: Sir Walter—er—did say that, but—ah—he—ah—but he added that he of course merely judged—er—this man Bassanio's feelings by his own in parting from his sister—"

" Did he say sister ?" cried Elizabeth.

" Well—no—not in those words," shuffled Kidd, perceiving quickly wherein his error lay, " but—ah—I jumped at the conclusion, seeing his intense enthusiasm for the lady's beauty and—er—intellectual qualities, that he referred to you, and it is from yourself that I have gained my knowledge as to the fraternal, not to say sororal, relationship that exists between you."

"That man's a diplomat from Diplomaville !" muttered Sir Henry Morgan, who, with Abeuchapeta and Conrad, was listening at the port without.

" He is that," said Abeuchapeta, " but he can't last much longer. He's perspiring like a pitcher of ice-water on a hot day, and a spirit of his size and volatile nature can't stand much of that without evaporating. If you will observe him closely you will see that his left arm already has vanished into thin air."

"By Jove !" whispered Conrad, "that's a fact ! If they don't let up on him he'll vanish. He's getting excessively tenuous about the top of his head."

All of which was only too true. Subjected to a scrutiny which he had little expected, the deceitful ambassador of the thieving band was rapidly dissipating, and, as those without had so fearsomely noted, was in imminent danger of complete sublimation, which, in the case of one possessed of so little elementary purity, meant nothing short of annihilation. Fortunately for Kidd, however, his wonderful tact had stemmed the tide of suspicion. Elizabeth was satisfied with his explanation, and in the minds of at least three of the most influential ladies on board, Portia, Xanthippe, and Elizabeth, he had become a creature worthy of credence, which meant that he had nothing more to fear.

"I am prepared, your Majesty," said Elizabeth, addressing Cleopatra, "to accept from this time on the gentleman's word. The little that he has already told us is hall-marked with truth. I should like to ask, however, one more question, and that is how our gentleman friends expected to embark us upon this voyage without letting us into the secret?"

"Oh, as for that," replied Kidd, with a deep-drawn sigh of relief, for he too had noticed the gradual evaporation of his arm and the incipient etherization of his cranium — "as for that, it was simple enough. There was to have been a day set apart for ladies' day at the club, and when you were all on board we were quietly to weigh anchor and start. The fact that you had anticipated the day, of your own volition, was telephoned by my scouts to me at my headquarters, and that news was by me transmitted by messenger to Sir Walter at Charon's Glen Island, where the long-talked-of fight between Samson and Goliath was taking place. Raleigh immediately replied, '*Good! Start at once. Paris first. Unlimited credit. Love to Elizabeth.*' Wherefore, ladies," he added, rising from his chair and walking to the door—"wherefore you are here and in my care. Make yourselves comfortable, and with the aid of the fashion papers which you have already received prepare yourselves for the joys that await you. With the aid of Madame Récamier and Baedeker's *Paris,* which you will find in the library, it will be your own fault if when you arrive there you resemble a great many less fortunate women who don't know what they want."

With these words Kidd disappeared through the door, and fainted in the arms of Sir Henry Morgan. The strain upon him had been too great.

"A charming fellow," said Portia, as the pirate disappeared.

"Most attractive," said Elizabeth.

"Handsome, too, don't you think?" asked Helen of Troy.

"And truthful beyond peradventure," observed Xanthippe, as she reflected upon the words the captain had attributed to Socrates. "I didn't believe him at first,

KIDD'S COMPANIONS ENDEAVORING TO RESTORE EVAPORATED POR-
TIONS OF HIS ANATOMY WITH A STEAM-ATOMIZER

but when he told me what my sweet-tempered philosopher had said, I was convinced."

"He's a sweet child," interposed Mrs. Noah, fondly. "One of my favorite grandchildren."

"Which makes it embarrassing for me to say," cried Cassandra, starting up angrily, "that he is a base caitiff!"

Had a bomb been dropped in the middle of the room, it could not have created a greater sensation than the words of Cassandra.

"What?" cried several voices at once. "A caitiff?"

"A caitiff with a capital K," retorted Cassandra. "I know that, because while he was telling his story I was listening to it with one ear and looking forward into the middle of next week with the other— I mean the other eye—and I saw—"

"Yes, you saw?" cried Cleopatra.

"I saw that he was deceiving us. Mark my words, ladies, he is a base caitiff," replied Cassandra—"a base caitiff."

"What did you see ?" cried Elizabeth, excitedly.

"This," said Cassandra, and she began a narration of future events which I must defer to the next chapter.   Meanwhile his associates were endeavoring to restore the evaporated portions of the prostrated Kidd's spirit anatomy by the use of a steam-atomizer, but with indifferent success.   Kidd's training had not fitted him for an intellectual combat with superior women, and he suffered accordingly.

X

A WARNING ACCEPTED

"IT is with no desire to interrupt my friend Cassandra unnecessarily," said Mrs. Noah, as the prophetess was about to narrate her story, "that I rise to beg her to remember that, as an ancestress of Captain Kidd, I hope she will spare a grandmother's feelings, if anything in the story she is about to tell is improper to be placed before the young. I have been so shocked by the stories of perfidy and baseness generally that have been published of late years, that I would interpose a protest while there is yet time if there is a line in Cassandra's story which ought to be withheld from the public; a protest based upon my affection for posterity, and in the interests of morality everywhere."

"You may rest easy upon that score, my dear Mrs. Noah," said the prophetess. "What I have to say would commend itself, I am sure, even to the ears of a British matron; and while it is as complete a demonstration of man's perfidy as ever was, it is none the less as harmless a little tale as the Dottie Dimple books or any other more recent study of New England character."

"Thank you for the load your words have lifted from my mind," said Mrs. Noah, settling back in her chair, a satisfied expression upon her gentle countenance. "I hope you will understand why I spoke, and withal why modern literature generally has been so distressful to me. When you reflect that the world is satisfied that most of man's criminal instincts are the result of heredity, and that Mr. Noah and I are unable to shift the responsibility for posterity to other shoulders than our own, you will understand my position. We were about the most domestic old couple that ever lived, and

when we see the long and varied assortment of crimes that are cropping out
everywhere in our descendants it is pain-
ful to us to realize what a pair of unconsciously wicked old fogies we must have
been."

"We all understand that," said Cleopatra, kindly; "and we are all prepared
to acquit you of any responsibility for the
advanced condition of wickedness to-day.
Man has progressed since your time, my
dear grandma, and the modern improve-
ments in the science of crime are no more
attributable to you than the invention of
the telephone or the oyster cocktail is
attributable to your lord and master."

"Thank you kindly," murmured the
old lady, and she resumed her knitting
upon a phantom tam - o' - shanter, which
she was making as a Christmas surprise
for her husband.

"When Captain Kidd began his story,"
said Cassandra, " he made one very bad
mistake, and yet one which was prompted
by that courtesy which all men instinctive-

ly adopt when addressing women. When he entered the room he removed his hat, and therein lay his fatal error, if he wished to convince me of the truth of his story, for with his hat removed I could see the workings of his mind. While you ladies were watching his lips or his eyes, some of you taking in the gorgeous details of his dress, all of you hanging upon his every word, I kept my eye fixed firmly upon his imagination, and I saw, what you did not, *that he was drawing wholly upon that!*"

"How extraordinary!" cried Elizabeth.

"Yes — and fortunate," said Cassandra. "Had I not done so, a week hence we should, every one of us, have been lost in the surging wickedness of the city of Paris."

"But, Cassandra," said Trilby, who was anxious to return once more to the beautiful city by the Seine, "he told us we were going to Paris."

"Of course he did," said Madame Récamier, "and in so many words. Certain-

" ' HE TOLD US WE WERE GOING TO PARIS ' "

ly he was not drawing upon his imagination there."

"And one might be lost in a very much worse place," put in Marguerite de Valois, "if, indeed, it were possible to lose us in Paris at all. I fancy that I know enough about Paris to find my way about."

"Humph!" ejaculated Cassandra. "What a foolish little thing you are! You don't imagine that the Paris of to-day is the Paris of your time, or even the Paris of that sweet child Trilby's time, do you? If you do you are very much mistaken. I almost wish I had not warned you of your danger and had let you go, just to see those eyes of yours open with amazement at the change. You'd find your Louvre a very different sort of a place from what it used to be, my dear lady. Those pleasing little windows through which your relations were wont in olden times to indulge in target practice at people who didn't go to their church are now kept closed; the galleries which used to swarm with people, many of whom ought.

11

to have been hanged, now swarm with
pictures, many of which ought not to have
been hung ; the romance which clung
about its walls is as much a part of the
dead past as yourselves, and were you to
materialize suddenly therein you would
find yourselves jostled and hustled and
trodden upon by the curious from other
lands, with Argus eyes taking in five hundred pictures a minute, and traversing
those halls at a rate of speed at which
Mercury himself would stand aghast."

" But my beloved Tuileries ?" cried
Marie Antoinette.

" Has been swallowed up by a play-
ground for the people, my dear," said Cassandra, gently. " Paris is no place for us,
and it is the intention of these men, in
whose hands we are, to take us there and
then desert us. Can you imagine anything worse than ourselves, the phantoms
of a glorious romantic past, basely desert-
ed in the streets of a wholly strange, su-
perficial, material city of to-day ? What
do you think, Elizabeth, would be your

fate if, faint and famished, you begged
for sustenance at an English door to-day,
and when asked your name and profession were to reply, ' Elizabeth, Queen of
England' ?"

"Insane asylum," said Elizabeth, shortly.

"Precisely.   So in Paris with the rest
of us," said Cassandra.

"How do you know all this ?" asked
Trilby, still unconvinced.

"I know it just as you knew how to
become a prima donna," said Cassandra.
"I am, however, my own Svengali, which
is rather preferable to the patent detach-
able hypnotizer you had. I hypnotize myself, and direct my mind into the future.
I was a professional forecaster in the days
of ancient Troy, and if my revelations had
been heeded the Priam family would, I
doubt not, still be doing business at the
old stand, and Mr. Æneas would not have
grown round-shouldered giving his poor
father a picky-back ride on the opening
night of the horse-show, so graphically
depicted by Virgil."

"I never heard about that," said Trilby. "It sounds like a very funny story,
though."

"Well, it wasn't so humorous for some
as it was for others," said Cassandra, with
a sly glance at Helen. "The fact is, until you mentioned it yourself, it never occurred to me that there was much fun in
any portion of the Trojan incident, ex-
cepting perhaps the delirium tremens of
old Laocoon, who got no more than he
deserved for stealing my thunder. I had
warned Troy against the Greeks, and they
all laughed at me, and said my eye to the
future was strabismatic ; that the Greeks
couldn't get into Troy at all, even if they
wanted to. And then the Greeks made a
great wooden horse as a gift for the Trojans, and when I turned my X-ray gaze
upon it I saw that it contained about six
brigades of infantry, three artillery regiments, and sharp-shooters by the score.
It was a sort of military Noah's Ark ; but
I knew that the prejudice against me was
so strong that nobody would believe what

I told them. So I said nothing. My prophecies never came true, they said, failing
to observe that my warning as to what
would be was in itself the cause of their
non-fulfilment. But desiring to save Troy,
I sent for Laocoon and told him all about
it, and he went out and announced it as
his own private prophecy ; and then, having tried to drown his conscience in strong
waters, he fell a victim to the usual ser-
pentine hallucination, and everybody said
he wasn't sober, and therefore unworthy
of belief. The horse was accepted, hauled into the city, and that night orders
came from hindquarters to the regiments
concealed inside to march. They march-
ed, and next morning Troy had been removed from the map ; ninety per cent.
of the Trojans died suddenly, and Æneas,
grabbing up his family in one hand and
his gods in the other, went yachting for
several seasons, ultimately settling down
in Italy. All of this could have been
avoided if the Trojans would have taken
the hint from my prophecies. They pre-

ferred, however, not to do it, with the
result that to-day no one but Helen and
myself knows even where Troy was, and
we'll never tell."

"It is all true," said Helen, proudly.
"I was the woman who was at the bottom
of it all, and I can testify that Cassandra
always told the truth, which is why she
was always so unpopular. When anything
that was unpleasant happened, after it was
all over she would turn and say, sweetly,
'I told you so.' She was the original 'I
told you so' nuisance, and of course she
had the newspapyruses down on her, because she never left them any sensation
to spring upon the public. If she had
only told a fib once in a while, the public
would have had more confidence in her."

"Thank you for your endorsement,"
said Cassandra, with a nod at Helen.
"With such testimony I cannot see how
you can refrain from taking my advice in
this matter ; and I tell you, ladies, that
this man Kidd has made his story up out
of whole cloth ; the men of Hades had no

more to do with our being here than we had ; they were as much surprised as we are to find us gone. Kidd himself was not aware of our presence, and his object in taking us to Paris is to leave us stranded there, disembodied spirits, vagrant souls with no familiar haunts to haunt, no place to rest, and nothing before us save perpetual exile in a world that would have no sympathy for us in our misfortune, and no belief in our continued existence."

"But what, then, shall we do ?" cried Ophelia, wringing her hands in despair.

"It is a terrible problem," said Cleopatra, anxiously ; "and yet it does seem as if our woman's instinct ought to show us some way out of our trouble."

"The Committee on Treachery," said Delilah, "has already suggested a chafing-dish party, with Lucretia Borgia in charge of the lobster Newberg."

"That is true," said Lucretia ; "but I find, in going through my reticule, that my maid, for some reason unknown to me,

has failed to renew my supply of poisons.
I shall discharge her on my return home,
for she knows that I never go anywhere
without them; but that does not help
matters at this juncture. The sad fact
remains that I could prepare a thousand
delicacies for these pirates without fatal
results."

"You mean immediately fatal, do you
not?" suggested Xanthippe. "I could myself prepare a cake which would in time
reduce our captors to a state of absolute
dependence, but of course the effect is not
immediate."

"We might give a musicale, and let
Trilby sing 'Ben Bolt' to them," suggested Marguerite de Valois, with a giggle.

"Don't be flippant, please," said Portia.
"We haven't time to waste on flippant
suggestions. Perhaps a court-martial of
these pirates, supplemented by a yard-arm,
wouldn't be a bad thing. I'll prosecute
the case."

"You forget that you are dealing with
immortal spirits," observed Cleopatra. "If

these creatures were mortals, hanging them
would be all right, and comparatively easy,
considering that we outnumber them ten
to one, and have many resources for getting them, more or less, in our power, but
they are not. They have gone through
the refining process of dissolution once,
and there's an end to that. Our only re-
source is in the line of deception, and if we
cannot deceive them, then we have ceased
to be women."

"That is truly said," observed Elizabeth. "And inasmuch as we have already
provided ourselves with a suitable committee for the preparation of our plans of
a deceptive nature, I move, as the easiest
possible solution of the difficulty for the
rest of us, that the Committee on Treachery be requested to go at once into executive session, with orders not to come
out of it until they have suggested a
plausible plan of campaign against our
abductors. We must be rid of them. Let
the Committee on Treachery say how."

"Second the motion," said Mrs. Noah.

" You are a very clear - headed young woman, Lizzie, and your grandmother is proud of you."

The Committee on Treachery were about to protest, but the chair refused to entertain any debate upon the question, which was put and carried with a storm of approval.

Five minutes later a note was handed through the port, addressed to Cleopatra, which read as follows :

" DEAR MADAME,—Six bells has just struck, and the officers and crew are hungry. Will you and your fair companions co-operate with us in our enterprise by having a hearty dinner ready within two hours ? A speck has appeared on the horizon which betokens a coming storm, else we would prepare our supper ourselves. As it is, we feel that your safety depends on our remaining on deck. If there is any beer on the ice, we prefer it to tea. Two cases will suffice.

" Yours respectfully,

" HENRY MORGAN, Bart., First Mate.'

" Hurrah !" cried Cleopatra, as she read this communication. " I have an idea.

"'YOU ARE A VERY CLEAR-HEADED YOUNG WOMAN, LIZZIE,' SAID MRS. NOAH"

Tell the Committttee on Treachery to appear before the full meeting at once."

The committee was summoned, and Cleopatra announced her plan of operation, and it was unanimously adopted; but what it was we shall have to wait for another chapter to learn.

XI

MAROONED

WHEN Captain Holmes arrived upon deck he seized his glass, and, gazing intently through it for a moment, perceived that the faithful Shem had not deceived him. Flying at half-mast from a rude, roughly hewn pole set upon a rocky height was the black flag, emblem of piracy, and, as Artemus Ward put it, "with the second joints reversed." It was in very truth a signal of distress.

"I make it a point never to be surprised," observed Holmes, as he peered through the glass, "but this beats me. I didn't know there was an island of this nature in these latitudes. Blackstone, go below and pipe Captain Cook on deck. Perhaps he knows what island that is."

"You'll have to excuse me, Captain Holmes," replied the Judge. "I didn't ship on this voyage as a cabin-boy or a messenger-boy. Therefore I—"

"Bonaparte, put the Judge in irons," interrupted Holmes, sternly. "I expect to be obeyed, Judge Blackstone, whether you shipped as a Lord Chief-Justice or a state-room steward. When I issue an order it must be obeyed. Step lively there, Bonaparte. Get his honor ironed and summon your marines. We may have work to do before night. Hamlet, pipe Captain Cook on deck."

"Aye, aye, sir," replied Hamlet, with alacrity, as he made off.

"That's the way to obey orders," said Holmes, with a scornful glance at Blackstone.

"I was only jesting, Captain," said the latter, paling somewhat.

"That's all right," said Holmes, taking up his glass again. "So was I when I ordered you in irons, and in order that you may appreciate the full force of the joke I repeat it.   Bonaparte, do your duty."

In an instant the order was obeyed, and the unhappy Judge shortly found himself manacled and alone in the forecastle.   Meanwhile Captain Cook, in response to the commander's order, repaired to the deck and scanned the distant coast.

"I can't place it," he said.   "It can't be Monte Cristo, can it ?"

"No, it can't," said the Count, who stood hard by.   "My island was in the Mediterranean, and even if it dragged anchor it couldn't have got out through the Strait of Gibraltar."

"Perhaps it's Robinson Crusoe's island," suggested Doctor Johnson.

"Not it," observed De Foe.   "If it is, the rest of you will please keep off.   It's mine, and I may want to use it again.   I've been having a number of interviews with Crusoe latterly, and he's given me a lot of new points, which I intend incorporating in a sequel for the *Cimmerian Magazine*."

"Well, in the name of Atlas, what island is it, then?" roared Holmes, angrily. "What is the matter with all you learned lubbers that I have brought along on this trip? Do you suppose I've brought you to whistle up favorable winds? Not by the beard of the Prophet! I brought you to give me information, and now when I ask for the name of a simple little island like that in plain sight there's not one of you able so much as to guess at it reasonably. The next man I ask for information goes into irons with Judge Blackstone if he doesn't answer me instantly with the information I want. Munchausen, what island is that?"

"Ahem! that?" replied Munchausen, trembling, as he reflected upon the Captain's threat. "What? Nobody knows what island that is? Why, you surprise me—"

"See here, Baron," retorted Holmes, menacingly, "I ask you a plain question, and I want a plain answer, with no evasions to gain time. Now it's irons or an answer. What island is that?"

"It's an island that doesn't appear on any chart, Captain," Munchausen responded instantly, pulling himself together for a mighty effort, "and it has never been given a name; but as you insist upon having one, we'll call it Holmes Island, in your honor. It is not stationary. It is a floating island of lava formation, and is a menace to every craft that goes to sea. I spent a year of my life upon it once, and it is more barren than the desert of Sahara, because you cannot raise even sand upon it, and it is devoid of water of any sort, salt or fresh."

"What did you live on during that year?" asked Holmes, eying him narrowly.

"Canned food from wrecks," replied the Baron, feeling much easier now that he had got a fair start—"canned food from wrecks, commander. There is a magnetic property in the upper stratum of this piece of derelict real estate, sir, which attracts to it every bit of canned substance that is lost overboard in all parts of the world. A ship is wrecked, say, in the Pacific Ocean, and ultimately all the loose metal upon her will succumb to the irresistible attraction of this magnetic upper stratum, and will find its way to its shores. So in any other part of the earth. Everything metallic turns up here sooner or later ; and when you consider that thousands of vessels go down every year, vessels which are provisioned with tinned foods only, you will begin to comprehend how many millions of pounds of preserved salmon, sardines, *pâté de foie gras*, peaches, and so on, can be found strewn along its coast."

"Munchausen," said Holmes, smiling, "by the blush upon your cheek, coupled with an occasional uneasy glance of the eye, I know that for once you are standing upon the, to you, unfamiliar ground of truth, and I admire you for it. There is nothing to be ashamed of in telling the truth occasionally. You are a man after

12

my own heart. Come below and have a cocktail. Captain Cook, take command of the *Gehenna* during my absence ; head her straight for Holmes Island, and when you discover anything new let me know. Bonaparte, in honor of Munchausen's remarkable genius I proclaim general amnesty to our prisoners, and you may release Blackstone from his dilemma ; and if you have any tin soldiers among your marines, see that they are lashed to the rigging. I don't want this electric island of the Baron's to get a grip upon my military force at this juncture."

With this Holmes, followed by Munchausen, went below, and the two worthies were soon deep in the mysteries of a phantom cocktail, while Doctor Johnson and De Foe gazed mournfully out over the ocean at the floating island.

" De Foe," said Johnson, " that ought to be a lesson to you. This realism that you tie up to is all right when you are alone with your conscience ; but when there are great things afoot, an im-

"'THAT OUGHT TO BE A LESSON TO YOU'"

agination and a broad view as to the
limitations of truth aren't at all bad.
You or I might now be drinking that
cocktail with Holmes if we'd only risen
to the opportunity the way Munchausen
did."

"That is true," said De Foe, sadly.
"But I didn't suppose he wanted that
kind of information. I could have spun
a better yarn than that of Munchausen's
with my eyes shut. I supposed he wanted
truth, and I gave it."

"I'd like to know what has become of
the House-boat," said Raleigh, anxiously
gazing through the glass at the island.
"I can see old Henry Morgan sitting down
there on the rocks with his elbows on his
knees and his chin in his hands, and Kidd
and Abeuchapeta are standing back of
him, yelling like mad, but there isn't a
boat in sight."

"Who is that man, off to the right,
dancing a fandango ?" asked Johnson.

"It looks like Conrad, but I can't tell.
He appears to have gone crazy. He's got

that wild look on his face which betokens insanity. We'll have to be careful in our parleyings with these people," said Raleigh.

"Anything new?" asked Holmes, returning to the deck, smacking his lips in enjoyment of the cocktail.

"No—except that we are almost within hailing distance," said Cook.

"Then give orders to cast anchor," observed Holmes. "Bonaparte, take a crew of picked men ashore and bring those pirates aboard. Take the three musketeers with you, and don't let Kidd or Morgan give you any back talk. If they try any funny business, exorcise them."

"Aye, aye, sir," replied Bonaparte, and in a moment a boat had been lowered and a sturdy crew of sailors were pulling for the shore. As they came within ten feet of it the pirates made a mad dash down the rough, rocky hillside and clamored to be saved.

"What's happened to you?" cried Bonaparte, ordering the sailors to back water,

"THE PIRATES MADE A MAD DASH DOWN THE ROUGH, ROCKY HILL-SIDE"

lest the pirates should too hastily board
the boat and swamp her.

"We are marooned," replied Kidd,
"and on an island of a volcanic nature.
There isn't a square inch of it that isn't
heated up to 125 degrees, and seventeen
of us have already evaporated. Conrad
has lost his reason; Abeuchapeta has become so tenuous that a child can see
through him. As for myself, I am growing iridescent with anxiety, and unless
I get off this infernal furnace I'll disappear like a soap-bubble. For Heav-
en's sake, then, General, take us off,
on your own terms. We'll accept anything."

As if in confirmation of Kidd's words,
six of the pirate crew collapsed and disappeared into thin air, and a glance at
Abeuchapeta was proof enough of his condition. He had become as clear as crystal,
and had it not been for his rugged outlines
he would hardly have been visible even to
his fellow-spirits. As for Kidd, he had
taken on the aspect of a rainbow, and it

was patent that his fears for himself were all too well founded.

Bonaparte embarked the leaders of the band first, returning subsequently for the others, and repaired with them at once to the *Gehenna,* where they were ushered into the presence of Sherlock Holmes. The first question he asked was as to the whereabouts of the House-boat.

" That we do not know," replied Kidd, mournfully, gazing downward at the wreck of his former self. " We came ashore, sir, early yesterday morning, in search of food. It appears that when—acting in a wholly inexcusable fashion, and influenced, I confess it, by motives of revenge—I made off with your club-house, I neglected to ascertain if it were well stocked with provisions, a fatal error; for when we endeavored to get supper we discovered that the larder contained but half a bottle of farcie olives, two salted almonds, and a soda cracker—not a luxurious feast for sixty-nine pirates and a hundred and eighty-three women to sit down to."

"That's all nonsense," said Demosthenes. "The House Committee had provided enough supper for six hundred people, in anticipation of the appetite of the members on their return from the fight."

"Of course they did," said Confucius; "and it was a good one, too—salads, salmon glacé, lobsters—every blessed thing a man can't get at home we had; and what is more, they'd been delivered on board. I saw to that before I went up the river."

"Then," moaned Kidd, "it is as I suspected. We were the victims of base treachery on the part of those women."

"Treachery? Well, I like that. Call it reciprocity," said Hamlet, dryly.

"We were informed by the ladies that there was nothing for supper save the items I have already referred to," said Kidd. "I see it all now. We had tried to make them comfortable, and I put myself to some considerable personal inconvenience to make them easy in their minds, but they were ungrateful."

"Whatever induced you to take 'em along with you ?" asked Socrates.

"We didn't want them," said Kidd. "We didn't know they were on board until it was too late to turn back. They'd broken in, and were having the club all to themselves in your absence."

"It served you good and right," said Socrates, with a laugh. "Next time you try to take things that don't belong to you, maybe you'll be a trifle more careful as to whose property you confiscate."

"But the House-boat—you haven't told us how you lost her," put in Raleigh, impatiently.

"Well, it was this way," said Kidd. "When, in response to our polite request for supper, the ladies said there was nothing to eat on board, something had to be done, for we were all as hungry as bears, and we decided to go ashore at the first port and provision. Unfortunately the crew got restive, and when this floating frying-pan loomed into view, to keep them good-natured we decided to land and see

if we could beg, borrow, or steal some sup-
plies. We had to. Observations taken
with the sextant showed that there was no
port within five hundred miles ; the island
looked as if it might be inhabited at least
by goats, and ashore we went, every man of
us, leaving the House-boat safely anchored
in the harbor. At first we didn't mind the
heat, and we hunted and hunted and hunted ; but after three or four hours I began to
notice that three of my sailors were shrivel-
ling up, and Conrad began to act as if he
were daft. Hawkins burst right before my
eyes. Then Abeuchapeta got prismatic
around the eyes and began to fade, and I
noticed a slight iridescence about myself ;
and as for Morgan, he had the misfortune
to lie down to take a nap in the sun, and
when he waked up, his whole right side
had evaporated. Then we saw what the
trouble was. We'd struck this lava island,
and were gradually succumbing to its intense heat. We rushed madly back to the
harbor to embark ; and our ship, gentlemen, and your House-boat, was slowly but

surely disappearing over the horizon, and flying from the flag-staff at the fore were signals of farewell, with an unfeeling P. S. below to this effect : ' *Don't wait up for us.   We may not be back until late.*' "

There was a pause, during which Socrates laughed quietly to himself, while Abeuchapeta and the one-sided Morgan wept silently.

" That, gentlemen of the Associated Shades, is all I know of the whereabouts of the House - boat," continued Captain Kidd.   " I have no doubt that the ladies practised a deception, to our discomfiture, and I must say that I think it was exceedingly clever—granting that it was desirable to be rid of us, which I don't, for we meant well by them, and they would have enjoyed themselves."

" But," cried Hamlet, " may they not now be in peril ?   They cannot navigate that ship."

" They got her out of the harbor all right," said Kidd.   " And I judged from the figure at the helm that Mrs. Noah had taken charge. What kind of a seaman she is I don't know."

"Almighty bad," ejaculated Shem, turning pale. "It was she who ran us ashore on Ararat."

" Well, wasn't that what you wanted ?" queried Munchausen.

"What we wanted!" cried Shem. "Well, I guess not. You don't want your yacht stranded on a mountain-top, do you ? She was a dead loss there, whereas if mother hadn't been in such a hurry to get ashore, we could have waited a month and landed on the seaboard."

" You might have turned her into a summer hotel," suggested Munchausen.

"Well, we must up anchor and away," said Holmes. " Our pursuit has merely begun, apparently. We must overtake this vessel, and the question to be answered is—where ?"

" That's easy," said Artemus Ward. " From what Shem says, I think we'd better look for her in the Himalayas."

"And, meanwhile, what shall be done with Kidd?" asked Holmes.

"He ought to be expelled from the club," said Johnson.

"We can't expel him, because he's not a member," replied Raleigh.

"Then elect him," suggested Ward.

"What on earth for?" growled Johnson.

"So that we can expel him," said Ward.

And while Boswell's hero was trying to get the value of this notion through his head, the others repaired to the deck, and the *Gehenna* was soon under way once more. Meanwhile Captain Kidd and his fellows were put in irons and stowed away in the forecastle, alongside of the water-cask in which Shylock lay in hiding.

XII

THE ESCAPE AND THE END

If there was anxiety on board of the *Gehenna* as to the condition and whereabouts of the House-boat, there was by no means less uneasiness upon that vessel itself. Cleopatra's scheme for ridding herself and her abducted sisters of the pirates had worked to a charm, but, having worked thus, a new and hitherto undreamed-of problem, full of perplexities bearing upon their immediate safety, now confronted them. The sole representative of a seafaring family on board was Mrs. Noah, and it did not require much time to see that her knowledge as to navigation was of an extremely primitive order, limited indeed to the science of floating.

When the last pirate had disappeared

behind the rocks of Holmes Island, and all was in readiness for action, the good old lady, who had hitherto been as calm and unruffled as a child, began to get red in the face and to bustle about in a manner which betrayed considerable perturbation of spirit.

"Now, Mrs. Noah," said Cleopatra, as, peeping out from the billiard-room window, she saw Morgan disappearing in the distance, "the coast is clear, and I resign my position of chairman to you. We place the vessel in your hands, and ourselves subject to your orders. You are in command. What do you wish us to do?"

"Very well," replied Mrs. Noah, putting down her knitting and starting for the deck. "I'm not certain, but I think the first thing to do is to get her moving. Do you know, I've never discovered whether this boat is a steamboat or a sailing-vessel? Does anybody know?"

"I think it has a naphtha tank and a propeller," said Elizabeth, "although I don't know. It seems to me my broth-

er Raleigh told me they'd had a naphtha
engine put in last winter after the freshet,
when the House-boat was carried ten
miles down the river, and had to be towed
back at enormous expense. They put it in
so that if she were carried away again she
could get back of her own power."

"That's unfortunate," said Mrs. Noah,
"because I don't know anything about
these new fangled notions. If there's any
one here who knows anything about
naphtha engines, I wish they'd speak."

"I'm of the opinion," said Portia, "that
I can study out the theory of it in a short
while."

"Very well, then," said Mrs. Noah,
"you can do it. I'll appoint you en-
gineer, and give you all your orders now,
right away, in advance. Set her going and
keep her going, and don't stop without a
written order signed by me. We might as
well be very careful, and have everything
done properly, and it might happen that
in the excitement of our trip you would
misunderstand my spoken orders and

make a fatal error. Therefore, pay no
attention to unwritten orders. That will
do for you for the present. Xanthippe,
you may take Ophelia and Madame Récamier, and ten other ladies, and, every
morning before breakfast, swab the larboard deck. Cassandra, Tuesdays you will
devote to polishing the brasses in the
dining-room, and the balance of your time
I wish you to expend in dusting the bric-
à-brac. Dido, you always were strong at
building fires. I'll make you chief stoker.
You will also assist Lucretia Borgia in the
kitchen. Inasmuch as the latter's maid
has neglected to supply her with the usual
line of poisons, I think we can safely en-
trust to Lucretia's hands the responsibilities of the culinary department."

"I'm perfectly willing to do anything
I can," said Lucretia, "but I must confess that I don't approve of your methods
of commanding a ship. A ship's captain
isn't a domestic martinet, as you are set-
ting out to be. We didn't appoint you
housekeeper."

"'NOW, MY CHILD,' SAID MRS. NOAH, FIRMLY, 'I DO NOT WISH ANY WORDS'"

"Now, my child," said Mrs. Noah,
firmly, "I do not wish any words. If I
hear any more impudence from you, I'll
put you ashore without a reference; and
the rest of you I would warn in all kind-
ness that I will not tolerate insubordina-
tion. You may, all of you, have one night
of the week and alternate Sundays off,
but your work must be done. The reg-
imen I am adopting is precisely that in
vogue on the Ark, only I didn't have the
help I have now, and things got into
very bad shape. We were out forty
days, and, while the food was poor and
the service execrable, we never lost a
life."

The boat gave a slight tremor.

"Hurrah," cried Elizabeth, clapping her
hands with glee, "we are off!"

"I will repair to the deck and get our
bearings," said Mrs. Noah, putting her
shawl over her shoulders. "Meantime,
Cleopatra, I appoint you first mate. See
that things are tidied up a bit here before
I return. Have the windows washed, and

13

to-morrow I want all the rugs and carpets taken up and shaken."

Portia meanwhile had discovered the naphtha engine, and, after experimenting several times with the various levers and stop-cocks, had finally managed to move one of them in such a way as to set the engine going, and the wheel began to re-volve.

"Are we going all right?" she cried, from below.

"I am afraid not," said the gallant com-mander. "The wheel is roiling up the water at a great rate, but we don't seem to be going ahead very fast—in fact, we're simply moving round and round as though we were on a pivot."

"I'm afraid we're aground amidships," said Xanthippe, gazing over the side of the House-boat anxiously. "She cer-tainly acts that way — like a merry-go-round."

"Well, there's something wrong, said Mrs. Noah; "and we've got to hurry and find out what it is, or those men will be back and we shall be as badly off as ever."

"Maybe this has something to do with it," observed Mrs. Lot, pointing to the anchor rope. "It looks to me as if those horrid men had tied us fast."

"That's just what it is," snapped Mrs. Noah. "They guessed our plan, and have fastened us to a pole or something, but I imagine we can untie it."

Portia, who had come on deck, gave a short little laugh.

"Why, of course we don't move," she said—"we are anchored!"

"What's that?" queried Mrs. Noah. "We never had an experience like that on the Ark."

Portia explained the science of the anchor.

"What nonsense!" ejaculated Mrs. Noah. "How can we get away from it?"

"We've got to pull it up," said Portia. "Order all hands on deck and have it pulled up."

"It can't be done, and, if it could, I

wouldn't have it !" said Mrs. Noah, indignantly. "The idea! Lifting heavy pieces
of iron, my dear Portia, is not a woman's
work. Send for Delilah, and let her cut
the rope with her scissors."

"It would take her a week to cut a
hawser like that," said Elizabeth, who had
been investigating. "It would be more
to the purpose, I think, to chop it in two
with an axe."

"Very well," replied Mrs. Noah, satisfied. "I don't care how it is done as long
as it is done quickly. It would never do
for us to be recaptured now."

The suggestion of Elizabeth was carried
out, and the queen herself cut the hawser
with six well-directed strokes of the axe.

"You *are* an expert with it, aren't
you ?" smiled Cleopatra.

"I am, indeed," replied Elizabeth, grim-
ly. "I had it suspended over my head
for so long a time before I got to the
throne that I couldn't help familiarizing
myself with some of its possibilities."

"Ah !" cried Mrs. Noah, as the vessel

began to move. "I begin to feel easier. It looks now as if we were really off."

"It seems to me, though," said Cleopatra, gazing forward, "that we are going backward."

"Oh, well, what if we are!" said Mrs. Noah. "We did that on the Ark half the time. It doesn't make any difference which way we are going as long as we go, does it?"

"Why, of course it does!" cried Elizabeth. "What can you be thinking of? People who walk backward are in great danger of running into other people. Why not the same with ships? It seems to me, it's a very dangerous piece of business, sailing backward."

"Oh, nonsense," snapped Mrs. Noah. "You are as timid as a zebra. During the Flood, we sailed days and days and days, going backward. It didn't make a particle of difference how we went—it was as safe one way as another, and we got just as far away in the end. Our main object now is to get away from the pirates, and that's what we are doing. Don't get emotional, Lizzie, and remember, too, that I am in charge. If I think the boat ought to go sideways, sideways she shall go. If you don't like it, it is still not too late to put you ashore."

The threat calmed Elizabeth somewhat, and she was satisfied, and all went well with them, even if Portia had started the propeller revolving reverse fashion ; so that the House-boat was, as Elizabeth had said, backing her way through the ocean.

The day passed, and by slow degrees the island and the marooned pirates faded from view, and the night came on, and with it a dense fog.

" We're going to have a nasty night, I am afraid," said Xanthippe, looking anxiously out of the port.

" No doubt," said Mrs. Noah, pleasantly. " I'm sorry for those who have to be out in it."

" That's what I was thinking about," observed Xanthippe. " It's going to be very hard on us keeping watch."

"Watch for what?" demanded Mrs. Noah, looking over the tops of her glasses at Xanthippe.

"Why, surely you are going to have lookouts stationed on deck?" said Elizabeth.

"Not at all," said Mrs. Noah. "Perfectly absurd. We never did it on the Ark, and it isn't necessary now. I want you all to go to bed at ten o'clock. I don't think the night air is good for you. Besides, it isn't proper for a woman to be out after dark, whether she's new or not."

"But, my dear Mrs. Noah," expostulated Cleopatra, "what will become of the ship?"

"I guess she'll float through the night whether we are on deck or not," said the commander. "The Ark did, why not this? Now, girls, these new-fangled yachting notions are all nonsense. It's night, and there's a fog as thick as a stone-wall all about us. If there were a hundred of you upon deck with ten eyes apiece, you couldn't see anything. You might much

better be in bed.   As your captain, chap-
eron, and grandmother, I command you
to stay below."

"But—who is to steer ?" queried Xanthippe.

"What's the use of steering until we
can see where to steer to ?" demanded
Mrs. Noah.   "I certainly don't intend
to bother with that tiller until some reason for doing it arises.   We haven't any
place to steer to yet ; we don't know where
we are going.   Now, my dear children,
be reasonable, and don't worry me.   I've
had a very hard day of it, and I feel my
responsibilities keenly.   Just let me man-
age, and we'll come out all right.   I've had
more experience than any of you, and
if—"

A terrible crash interrupted the old
lady's remarks.   The House-boat shivered
and shook, careened way to one side, and
as quickly righted and stood still.   A mad
rush up the gangway followed, and in a
moment a hundred and eighty-three pale-
faced, trembling women stood upon the

"A GREAT HELPLESS HULK TEN FEET TO THE REAR"

deck, gazing with horror at a great helpless hulk ten feet to the rear, fastened by
broken ropes and odd pieces of rigging
to the stern-posts of the House-boat, sink-
ing slowly but surely into the sea.

It was the *Gehenna!*

The House-boat had run her down and
her last hour had come, but, thanks to
the stanchness of her build and wonderful beam, the floating club-house had
withstood the shock of the impact and
now rode the waters as gracefully as
ever.

Portia was the first to realize the extent
of the catastrophe, and in a short while
chairs and life - preservers and tables—
everything that could float—had been
tossed into the sea to the struggling im-
mortals therein. On board the *Gehenna,*
those who had not cast themselves into
the waters, under the cool direction of
Holmes and Bonaparte, calmly lowered the
boats, and in a short while were not only
able to felicitate themselves upon their
safety, but had likewise the good fortune

to rescue their more impetuous brethren
who had preferred to swim for it. Ultimately, all were brought aboard the
House-boat in safety, and the men in
Hades were once more reunited to
their wives, daughters, sisters, and *fiancées*, and Elizabeth had the satisfaction
of once more saving the life of Raleigh
by throwing him her ruff as she had done
a year or so previously, when she and her
brother had been upset in the swift cur-
rent of the river Styx.

Order and happiness being restored,
Holmes took command of the House-
boat and soon navigated her safely back
into her old-time berth. The *Gehenna*
went to the bottom and was never seen
again, and when the roll was called it
was found that all who had set out upon
her had returned in safety save Shylock,
Kidd, Sir Henry Morgan, and Abeuchapeta ; but even they were not lost, for, five
weeks later, these four worthies were
found early one morning drifting slowly
up the river Styx, gazing anxiously out

from the top of a water-cask and yelling
lustily for help.

And here endeth the chronicle of the
pursuit of the good old House - boat.
Back to her moorings, the even tenor of
her ways was once more resumed, but
with one slight difference.

The ladies became eligible for membership, and, availing themselves of the privilege, began to think less and less of the
advantages of being men and to rejoice
that, after all, they were women ; and even
Xanthippe and Socrates, after that night
of peril, reconciled their differences, and
no longer quarrel as to which is the more
entitled to wear the toga of authority.
It has become for them a divided skirt.

As for Kidd and his fellows, they have
never recovered from the effects of their
fearful, though short, exile upon Holmes
Island, and are but shadows of their
former shades ; whereas Mr. Sherlock
Holmes has so endeared himself to his
new - found friends that he is quite as
popular with them as he is with us, who

have yet to cross the dark river and be subjected to the scrutiny of the Committee on Membership at the House-boat on the Styx.

Even Hawkshaw has been able to detect his genius.

THE END